UK L.

THE WINTER

Chris Harris

Copyright © Chris Harris 2022

The author's moral rights have been asserted.
All rights reserved. No part of this publication may be reproduced, stored in or introduced into a retrieval system or transmitted in any form or by any means, electronic, mechanical, photocopying, recording or otherwise without prior written permission from the publisher.

This novel is entirely a work of fiction. Names, characters, places and incidents are either the product of the author's imagination or are used fictitiously, and any resemblance to any person or persons, living or dead, is entirely coincidental. No affiliation is implied or intended to any organisation or recognisable body mentioned within.

First published by DHP Publishing in 2017
Published by Vulpine Press in the United Kingdom in 2022

ISBN: 978-1-83919-134-3

www.vulpine-press.com

CHAPTER ONE

Shadowy figures in black and white. Whiteness all around me. Screams from Becky? Cold, cold snow on my face, then nothing...

Slowly, bit by bit, the nightmare receded and relief flooded through me. Just a dream, I told myself. All just a bad dream.

I began to wake up.

As my senses returned to me, everything swam back into focus. I was lying in my own bed.

Confusion took hold. Why was I here? And more importantly, why did my head feel as if it had gone ten rounds with Frank Bruno? I closed my eyes against the slicing pain and drifted off again.

Seconds (or hours?) later I started to come round again. "What's going on?" I croaked. Why was my throat so dry? The last thing I remembered was – "Oh my God! Becky!"

My eyes shot open as the memories came flooding back and panic seized me. Almost immediately, I heard a familiar voice.

"It's OK, darling. I'm here; we're all here. We're all safe. Just lie still now. Jerry's on his way."

"Becky, is that you?" My throat was so hoarse I had trouble speaking. "What happened? The last thing I remember is you..."

I broke off and the tears came. I remembered how desperate I'd been, fighting to get through the snow, as I watched that bastard hit my wife and bundle her into the back of the armoured car.

"He shot me as I was trying to reach you, didn't he? I'm sorry Becky. I tried to get to you. I let you down. I should have been there to protect you." The tears came thick and fast.

Shaking her head gently, Becky took my hand in hers, "Tom, it's fine, honestly. We'll tell you everything that's happened soon, but the important thing is we're all OK. You did your best and what happened was my fault, not yours…"

She was interrupted by Stanley and Daisy bursting into the room, closely followed by a smiling Jerry.

At the sight of me, they stopped in their tracks and hung back, not sure if it was OK to approach the bed.

"Come here, you pair," I croaked again. My throat still felt raw and dry and I coughed a little. I desperately needed a drink, just to soothe it.

Reassured, they both rushed forward. As I moved my head, I realised with a shock that it was swathed in bandages. I hugged them both with one arm and using my free hand, touched my head tentatively.

"Tom, don't fiddle," Jerry said gently.

A few minutes later, Becky ushered the kids out of the room, telling them that Daddy needed some rest.

With Jerry's help, I managed to sit upright. Becky handed me a glass of water and I sipped it gratefully, my throat immediately feeling better.

Jerry watched me carefully for a moment or two.

"We were a bit worried about you for a while, Tom."

"Why?" I asked. "How long have I been here?"

"Five days!" I exclaimed when he told me.

Jerry nodded, "Becky hasn't left your side since we got her back four days ago. She refused to go anywhere."

I looked at Becky properly for the first time. She looked an absolute wreck. She had two black eyes, which were beginning to fade, and her hair was in disarray. And although freshly laundered clothes were a thing of the past now, it was clear that she'd been wearing the same things for some days.

Cold fury hit me.

"I hope they got the bastard who did that to you."

"Yes," said Becky calmly, "but don't worry about that for the moment; you're back with us now and that's the main thing. Let Jerry check you over and then we'll bring you up to date."

Jerry lost no time in examining me. With the limited equipment he had available to him, it was a very "low-tech" process.

He checked my eyesight and focus, reflexes and memory, and after some general prodding and poking, announced that I should be OK, but I was lucky to be alive.

Unwrapping the bandages that were covering my head, he proceeded to explain my injuries to me.

"You've been shot in the only place they couldn't hurt you too badly," he said, smiling, "in the head!"

Now that the bandages had been removed, he held up a mirror. I had a wound dressing on the right-hand side of my forehead. Asking me to hold the mirror, he carefully peeled off the dressing.

I had a livid gash running from my forehead to below my ear. My hair had been shaved. It was an ugly, deep wound.

"No bloody wonder my head hurts!" I said.

Jerry grinned and shook his head, "If the lottery was still running, I'd tell you to go and buy a ticket. Less than a quarter of an inch to the right and you wouldn't be here now.

The bullet grazed your skull and went as deep as it could, without actually touching anything vital. You've been unconscious since it happened, so all we could do was hope and pray that you'd come back to us once your brain had sorted itself out, after being rattled a bit by the bullet."

Still looking at myself, I said, "You put it so well."

Jerry turned serious, "If you'd remained unconscious any longer, we were planning to transfer you back to the base, where they could run more tests on you to try to work out the extent of the damage to your brain. But you began to move slightly yesterday and respond to our voices, so we knew you were coming back to us. We removed the tubes that were giving you fluids and medicines this morning to prevent you from doing any further damage to yourself."

I shifted restlessly, "Can I get up yet?"

"No, Tom." He smiled. "Let's leave that till tomorrow. You may feel all right while you're lying down but trust me, you're not back to your old self yet. If you get up, fall over and bang your head, we'll most likely be back to square one. One more day in bed won't do you any harm."

I pulled a face but in fact had no trouble drifting off to sleep again.

The next time I woke I could see light streaming through a gap in the curtains. Looking round, I saw Becky slumped asleep in a chair in the corner of the room. She was still wearing the same clothes and obviously hadn't left me. How long had I been out for this time?

I felt much better. My head still hurt like crazy but I felt more with it. I looked over at Becky. In spite of her weariness, she looked beautiful to me.

Her soft brown hair, much longer now that visits to the hairdressers were a thing of the past, covered half her face, making her bruises less visible. As if sensing my scrutiny, she opened her eyes, raised her head and smiled at me. I smiled back.

I was reminded that she always seemed to know when the children were about to stir, and would wake up just before them.

Hearing a quiet snore, I looked over the side of the bed. Stanley and Daisy were fast asleep under the same duvet on a mattress on the floor.

"They both wanted to be here when you woke up."

"How long have I been asleep?"

"All night again," she said, stretching and yawning. "Jerry says it's a good sign. Your body's healing itself, so sleep is good."

"I do feel a lot better now," I admitted. "I felt a bit fuzzy and discombobulated yesterday. Now it's just my head that hurts."

We were speaking in whispers so as not to wake the kids. Becky got up from her chair, lay down next to me on the bed, and we waited for them to wake up.

An hour later, with Becky and Stanley supporting me as my legs still felt unsteady, we all walked downstairs.

As I entered the kitchen, to my utter embarrassment, everyone crowded round me clapping and cheering.

CHAPTER TWO

Touched by everyone's genuine show of affection and concern for me, I motioned for them to be quiet, sat down gratefully on the proffered chair and accepted a cup of coffee from my sister, Jane. She gave me a fierce hug and a kiss on the cheek as she handed it to me.

Realising that I was absolutely starving, and completely ignoring Jerry's advice about not eating too much, I proceeded to wolf down everything that was put in front of me.

Becky had already told me not to ask how she, Michelle and Kim had come to be rescued. She'd assured me that they'd all been rescued safely, but had insisted that it would be best if everyone involved was present when the story was told. The wait would be worth it. I managed to restrain myself and kept the conversation to "road business".

The house began to feel crowded as more people arrived. As Harry entered, he made straight for Kim and gave her a kiss on both cheeks before turning to me and shaking my hand.

"Glad you're OK, Tom," he said, and I was touched by his sincerity. "You had us worried there! Your family's putting the military to shame. First your wife who, by the way, commands more respect among the men than any beaten up old sergeant, and now you! Single-handedly leaping barricades, rescuing my men under fire and then leading the charge against the enemy…"

Pausing for breath, he added, "Can you stop it, please, you're making us look bad."

I laughed. "Thanks Harry. But I did get shot, you know!"

He shrugged and grinned, "Occupational hazard when you run blindly at the enemy with nothing more than a strongly worded letter, I'm afraid. I never said it was the smartest thing to do; just the bravest."

"Well, with the greatest respect," I countered, "I was trying to rescue my wife and therefore, being brave didn't really come into it. Someone was hurting her and I just wanted to rip their heads off."

He glanced over at Kim and said quietly, "There's no greater deed than rescuing the one you love."

Looking up at the same moment, Kim must have heard at least part of what he said, because she blushed, smiled at him and then looked away again.

What had I missed in the five days I'd been unconscious?

Allan, accompanied by Michelle, Bob, Russ and his wife Jo, closely followed by Chris Garland and Pete (brandishing his notepad as always), now squeezed into the kitchen, which was threatening to burst at the seams.

Pete assumed control by raising his fingers to his mouth and emitting a shrill whistle.

"Can we all quieten down for a moment please!" He paused, waiting for the volume to lower, before resuming.

"If everyone could go and start their tasks for the day, please. Poor Tom here needs a moment with a few of us, because I believe he'll need to be brought up to speed on what's recently happened."

The room slowly emptied, as most of the adults went out to start work, and the children, somewhat more reluctantly, all trooped down the road to report for their morning lessons with Mary and Mandy.

Unable to contain myself any longer, I burst out, "Can someone please just tell me what the hell happened? It's killing me! Just bloody tell me, please!"

Becky squeezed my hand in an attempt to calm me down.

Harry looked round at us all and began.

"Shall I start? If anyone wants to join in, then please, feel free to butt in."

This was his story.

He'd been stationed at the other barricade when the first shots were fired. Following the agreed protocol, he'd stayed at his post and made sure that everyone was on full alert and ready for action. After a few minutes, having satisfied himself that his station was secure now that more residents had arrived to reinforce the defenders, and aware that gunfire was still erupting from the direction of the other barricade, he'd made his way over there.

The place was in chaos.

Nobody appeared to have any idea what was happening except that the gunfire had now ceased. Most people were crouching behind the barricades, trying to make sense of the situation, while the rest were furiously trying to administer first aid to Dave and the soldier. It soon became clear that they were beyond help.

Reports of the sound of a vehicle engine and shouting from further up the road, only served to increase the confusion.

Eventually, after a shouted exchange to establish that the two soldiers who could be seen sheltering behind the wall were friendly, and therefore safe to approach, Harry, Allan and Russ made their way up to them.

The soldiers quickly pointed out where I was lying and Jerry was sent for. Once he'd ascertained that I was still alive, he sent for help and I was hastily carried back for urgent treatment.

In the meantime, the two soldiers quickly explained what had happened.

Once everyone had recovered from the shock of the attackers coming from among us, the planning began. Contact was made with Captain Berry, but this placed him in a difficult position. All his men were occupied in forming a cordon around the farmhouse, and he was worried that that any sudden activity might prematurely announce their presence, putting more lives in danger. However, realising the urgency of our situation, he quickly promised to dispatch any troops he could safely extricate from their current positions, back to us. Despite this, from our point of view it would still be several hours before they got to us. As Harry had been left with just five soldiers, one of whom was injured and another of whom was dead, we were more or less on our own.

As things stood, one of the members of our small community had been killed and three others had been taken. They had to get them back, but the kidnappers had taken the last vehicle. The only other vehicles available were the lorries, which would be next to useless in such deep snow.

The tracks made by the fleeing vehicle had left a clear trail, but on foot a rescue party would stand no chance. It was only when Jerry (who had arrived to give everyone an update on my condition) reminded everyone that I had a Land Rover sitting in my garage, that the plan began to take shape.

Russ and one of the soldiers with mechanical experience immediately left to check it out. Shortly afterwards, they returned and confirmed that they'd found the parts I'd removed to disable it, and that it would take them about thirty minutes to re-attach them and get the vehicle started. This was better news.

The rescue party was hastily assembled, consisting of Harry, Allan, Chris and two of the remaining soldiers.

At the mention of Chris, I stopped Harry and said, "But Chris, your ankle? You didn't have to do that. Someone else could have gone."

Chris grinned wryly, "Yes I know that. And trust me, there was no shortage of volunteers, but let's face it, my knowledge of tracking and hunting's a useful skill. They still weren't happy about taking me, so I really had to apply the pressure to get them to agree. In the end, I laid it on a bit heavy about how I was single etc. so if something went wrong, then most of the others would be leaving behind widows and children, and I wouldn't."

Pete clapped him on the back. "He can be very persuasive when he wants to be!"

I nodded at Chris, and Harry continued.

Once the Land Rover was in working order and fully fuelled, with a few extra jerrycans of fuel strapped to the roof rack, the five heavily armed rescuers set off.

Back at the base, Colonel Moore had now been appraised of the situation, and had given orders for the drone that had been monitoring Captain Berry and his men to be redeployed to help our party find its quarry.

As the Land Rover followed the tracks in the snow, which showed up clearly in the bright moonlight, constant three-way radio communication was maintained between the car, the base and the road. Everyone's attention had shifted from the attack at the farmhouse to the rescue attempt.

Inside the car, the mood was tense. The fact that Kim and Michelle had been taken must have been hard on Harry and Allan. I remembered my own furious struggle to get to Becky, and realised that it must have taken all their self-control not to drive as fast as possible to get to them. Instead, the party pressed on steadily. A tactical and cautious approach was needed now.

The bright moonlight reflecting off the white blanket of snow made it unnecessary to use the headlights on the car. The rescue party moved on.

After three agonisingly frustrating hours, the UAV operator reported that she'd picked up a heat signal from a vehicle ahead.

It had to be them.

After following the UAV operator's directions until they got there, everyone stepped from the Land Rover and cautiously approached the armoured car, weapons at the ready.

It was lying empty and abandoned in a ditch. Somehow the driver had managed to make a mistake, and had driven it straight into a deep ditch that ran parallel to the road.

In spite of the vehicle's four-wheel drive system and heavy duty off-road tyres, it had proved impossible to get it out of the ditch. The quagmire of snow and mud around the vehicle, churned up by spinning tyres, was a testament to their frantic efforts to do so.

Footprints and drag marks led away across the fields. The armoured car's engine was cool now so it had been there for a while, but Chris was reassuring. Even with a head start of several hours, it wouldn't be possible for them to travel far in such conditions, especially if the women were not being cooperative. And yet the

UAV, with all its high-tech equipment, could find no trace of them.

All they could do was start tracking them on foot.

Thankfully, the trail proved easy to follow. After a quick discussion, they concluded that the fleeing men probably weren't expecting any pursuit, as they believed they'd stolen the only useable vehicle remaining to us. Encouraged by this thought, the rescuers picked up the pace, only exercising caution when approaching walls or hedges.

Finally, they were rewarded by the sound of muffled shouts and screams in the distance. They picked up their speed even more, spurred on by the knowledge that they were close.

The trail led to a barn standing in the middle of a field. After cautiously circling the building, they discovered that the only door into the building was closed. One of the soldiers crept forward, covered by everyone else, who held their weapons ready. It was locked or barred from the inside.

The shouts from the men inside the building, and the screams and shouts of defiance from the three women, painted a clear picture of what the men were trying to do.

There was barely any time to think. They had to find a way into the barn. The door looked sturdy so they rejected the idea of trying to barge through. The men inside could not be given an opportunity to do the women any more harm, or prepare to defend themselves. As far as they knew, all three were armed with shotguns or automatic weapons. They could not be allowed the time to use them.

A frantic search revealed a loose corrugated sheet that had been used to repair a hole in one of the walls of the barn. Using a knife, the nails holding the sheet in place were quickly but quietly extracted and the sheet removed to reveal a hole large enough to crawl through.

The scene inside, lit by a single propane lantern, was harrowing. The men had all three women pinned down, and were careless of how much they were hurting them.

The women, scratched and bruised and their clothes torn, were furiously fighting to get away. Filled with rage, the rescuers launched their attack.

Outnumbered and caught off guard, the would-be rapists didn't stand a chance. Before long they were beaten unconscious and tied up on the floor.

Harry paused in the telling of his story and looked a little uncomfortable, as if unsure about what to say next.

I broke the silence, "What happened then?"

Harry opened his mouth to say something, and then Michelle spoke up. Eyes shining with tears, but looking me straight in the eye, she said firmly, "I killed them!"

The simple statement hung in the air for a moment, then she gathered herself and continued. "I made myself a promise that after what happened to us at St Agnes Road, no one would ever do that to me again." She glanced at Kim at this point, "And I'll do anything I can to stop it happening to anyone else. No one should have to go through that!"

I closed my eyes, thinking about what might have happened to Becky.

Wiping her eyes but lifting her head defiantly, she continued, "They were guilty. We saw them kill our people. I don't think they planned to kidnap us; we were just in the wrong place at the wrong time.

I'm sure if we'd been men on the barricade, they would have just killed us there and then. But they took us by surprise, and before we knew it we'd been beaten and thrown into the back of a truck. Then they bound our arms and legs to stop us escaping."

She looked at Becky and Kim and her voice hardened, "No one else was involved. Our men left them tied up on the ground. I waited until everyone was outside, and then before anyone could stop me, I picked up one of their rifles and shot each of them in the head."

Allan put his arm around her in support and she responded by gently touching his arm, before saying quietly, "I'd do it again in an instant. We can't rely on anyone else to administer justice for us and I wouldn't want someone else to do my dirty work for me."

The room was silent for a moment, and then Pete cleared his throat and spoke up.

"Michelle, we're all a hundred percent behind you and what you did. We're just sad that you had to do it. Everyone fully supports Colonel Moore's new constitution."

Becky spoke for the first time. "If you hadn't done it, I would have," she said firmly. "Those bastards were pure evil. They could have satisfied themselves with just stealing the vehicle and some supplies, and then disappearing, and that would have been the end of it. Instead, they murdered poor Dave and Private Mclean for their weapons, and abducted us because we happened to be there."

People nodded in agreement. At this moment, Paul Berry walked into the room and the mood lifted a little. He apologised for his late arrival, explaining that he'd been on the radio to the base at Hereford. He took in the situation at a glance.

"Michelle, if you hadn't done it then, there would have been a queue, trust me," he said. "And while their motives may not seem logical to us, it's proved that we can't trust anyone until we know them well enough. Because of their actions, we've had to change the policy and procedures we were putting in place at the base. The fact that those three men were in such close proximity to senior government officials and royalty has scared the hell out of our security people."

He looked round at us all and added, "Sorry, have I interrupted?"

I shook my head. "No, not at all. I think they've covered everything I needed to know. Michelle, I can guarantee that no one will ever think badly of you for what you did. In my opinion, you're one of the bravest women I know. Those bastards deserved to die, and you did it without hesitation or any expectation of someone else doing it.

Right, Paul," I said, turning to him expectantly. "Now you're here, you can tell me about the attack on the farm."

CHAPTER THREE

Paul looked round at us all for a moment, as if deciding what to say. "Not much to report, really. The mission was a complete success. The missiles did their job, and most of the ones who were left alive were too shocked and disorientated to put up much resistance. A few of them tried to fight back, but they didn't last long against the kind of firepower we had."

"Did you find out where they came from?" I asked.

He nodded coldly. "Yes. We kept a few of them alive for a short while so they could be questioned."

It was as he'd suspected. A lot of them had come from the military prison at Colchester. Not long after the event, most of the prisoners had been released, as the prison no longer had the resources to continue feeding and looking after them. But quite a few were deemed too dangerous to be let out and to their credit, the few remaining Military Provost staff had stayed on to guard them.

At some point, a mistake had been made, and the prisoners had managed to escape and kill the guards. From that time, they'd embarked on a campaign of destruction and intimidation, killing and stealing from everyone they encountered. Their numbers had increased as "like-minded" degenerates were spared execution, (a fate handed out to most of the unfortunates they met) and opted to join them instead.

Their plan was simple: they would move from group to group, attacking and destroying anyone who got in their way, and living off the captured supplies until they found somewhere suitable for a permanent base.

"Did you get them all?" I asked.

Paul nodded. "We believe so, yes. We counted over forty bodies and recovered a fair number of weapons and supplies from the building the missiles destroyed. No one could have got through the cordon we put up around the farmhouse. The threat they posed to the region has been permanently extinguished."

The conversation in the room descended into general chitchat for a while, until I recollected Paul's comment about the change to policies and procedures at the Hereford base. As I asked about this the room hushed again, as people stopped to listen.

"Well," he said, "after the event, as you know, we were only allowing people we regarded as completely trustworthy on to the base to live among us. But after contact was made with you here and we discovered what fantastic progress you'd made, and realised that your achievements were putting the government's efforts to shame…well, the meetings you had with the hierarchy made an enormous difference. So then we began to adopt a more outward-looking and proactive approach."

I nodded, wondering where this was going.

"As I said before," he continued, "the fact that those three men were living among us for a time and had close contact and even conversations with some very important people…well, it's made a lot of people very nervous and led to a reassessment of the situation…"

He could see the agitation building up on my face and held up his hand, "Please, Tom, let me finish, and listen to everything I have to say before you start judging us."

I subsided for the moment and let him speak.

"For security reasons, a temporary ban has been placed on allowing new arrivals into the base. This doesn't mean we're going to stop helping people; it just means that they won't be allowed full access to all the facilities we can offer. Also, all arrivals since the event will be subject to further screening. We're devising various new methods with whatever expertise and equipment we have available."

Noting the shocked looks on most of our faces, he added with a laugh, "No, it's not what you think, we're not going to be waterboarding people or anything like that! One thing we are trying to do is to get an old polygraph machine, (a lie detector, in other words) that we've found, calibrated and working again. We're also putting together enhanced interview and background checking procedures.

It's become clear that the systems we have in place aren't sufficient and need changing. It's just unfortunate that it took such a disturbing event to highlight the fact."

He paused and looked round at us all before continuing, "After careful consideration, the outreach and relief programme we were planning will have to be scaled back for a time, as our priority for the moment is to concentrate on securing all the known locations of large quantities of stored weapons. We can't risk any other groups like the one we've just put down finding them.

As you can imagine, there are a lot of places we need to reach. It's not just military bases we need to think about; the police also had a sizeable arsenal spread around the UK. In hindsight, this should have been done immediately after the event, but we just followed the protocol set out, and to our shame, allowed ourselves to be cocooned in our nice safe bunker…" He broke off for a moment, looking sombre, then carried on.

"Still," he said, slightly more cheerfully, "we can't change the past, we can only influence the future. The one benefit from all this is that we'll be embarking on missions much further out than we'd initially planned. Every mission will be given the same instructions: make contact and see what help we can offer to every group or individual we come across.

We won't be skulking around at night anymore; the patrols will make themselves as visible as possible and be on the lookout for survivors."

Once again, he paused and his smile disappeared. "But what I will say is, if you're picturing our patrols arriving with flags waving and carnivals and bands, then you're mistaken. It's only two weeks since we were attacked on patrol, and we narrowly escaped being taken out by the group we've just eliminated. Basic security protocols will be followed at all times until we're certain that whatever group we've encountered is peaceful." He grinned wryly and added, "We may not initially look too friendly, but in my opinion, military vehicles were designed to look intimidating and there's not much we can change about that.

"Once the mission commander is satisfied of a group's legitimacy, all the help and advice we have available will be offered to them. Initially we'll offer food and medical assistance if required. We'll also bring them up to speed on what's happened to this country and the rest of the world, and then we'll ask them if they want to be part of the plan the government is formulating to help rebuild the UK. I know we've been over this before with you all, but once contact has been made and we've ascertained that they agree with the country's new constitution, we'll continue our mission to secure the weapons.

We'll make a note of their location and we'll promise to maintain contact with them, but other than that we won't be able to offer any guarantees about when we'll be able to return. Hopefully, knowing that they're not on their own will make a big difference to them."

I thought about what he'd said. It made sense. None of us wanted to have to deal with any more gangs armed to the teeth, so a plan to secure weapons seemed sensible. A thought occurred to me. "So what would you do if you came across another group like us? One that was friendly but had military weapons. Would you take the weapons away from them?"

To my relief, Paul shook his head firmly, "Absolutely not. That would be the quickest way to alienate them. We'd be taking away their only means of protection. Look, none of the procedures have been finalised yet, but I can assure you that if a group is friendly, no questions will be asked. But if, on the other hand, they prove to be hostile, then we'll be taking their weapons, whether they like it or not." Looking grim, he added, "Logic dictates that Gumin and those renegade soldiers can't be the only rotten apples in the barrel, so I guess we'll have to be prepared for more violence."

At this point, Jerry intervened and told everyone I'd done enough for today. The meeting broke up. I would have complained but was dismayed to find that I was feeling weak and exhausted again.

I knew I was going to hate being the patient, but Jerry had already told me in no uncertain terms that I was incredibly lucky;

firstly, to be alive and secondly, to have come through the experience without apparently suffering any permanent damage.

He told me he was putting me on a week's bed and house rest and that, aside from family members, I would only be allowed to have short meetings with everyone else. Becky put a stop to my protestations by promising severe future marital sanctions if I didn't comply. The only course of action left was to give in. However, congratulating myself on my cunning, I resolved to become the most difficult, demanding patient ever, in the hope that they would become so exasperated with me, they would release me from my incarceration.

It didn't work.

CHAPTER FOUR

As the days dragged on, the weather was increasingly becoming an issue. It was colder than anyone could remember and snow storm after snow storm hit, adding layer upon layer to the snow already piled up in deep drifts against the windows. The world outside was silent; a freezing wilderness enveloped in a white blanket.

The freezing conditions curtailed a lot of the outdoor work in the road, so most people were re-allocated to tasks involving internal house improvements, or were given duties that could take place within the shelter of the kitchen area.

As we worked, we talked about the weather. Could it be a coincidence that the harshest winter on record by a long way was happening so soon after the world's power had been turned off? No more gases from factories, cars and homes being pumped out into the atmosphere.

Surely this meant the end of global warming? The theory bounced back and forth between us, and even though the experts back at the base argued against it, referring to the legendary "winter of 1947" as proof that a harsh winter can come out of nowhere, most of us weren't convinced.

Travel either by car or on foot was severely hampered by the continual falls of snow. For the sake of people's safety, travel between the road and the base was suspended. An attempt to recover the stolen armoured car from its ditch had proved how dangerous conditions were, because the army engineers had almost managed to get the entire fleet stuck in the attempt (a fact which had been a source of great amusement to the rest of the troops).

The houses in the road were full to bursting point, as the replacements who had arrived with the convoy were obliged to bunk up with the soldiers they were supposed to be replacing.

Despite this, the troops remained cheerful, willingly pitching in to help the residents with their chores, and rarely complaining about their overcrowded accommodation. From their point of view, they knew that their families were safe and warm back in Herefordshire, and in the meantime, they were glad to be doing something rather than kicking their heels at the base. From time to time they moaned and griped as any good squaddie would, but for the most part, they threw themselves into their work with gusto.

Foraging parties were also cancelled and foot patrols were limited to the area immediately surrounding the compound. Even then, they kept to a set route so that any new tracks from strangers could easily be identified.

So apart from guard duties and essential maintenance, we hunkered down and endured and kept ourselves as busy as possible.

Not that this was much of a hardship; thanks to all the work we'd put in previously, fitting log burners, reinstating fireplaces and using gas heaters, the houses remained reasonably warm and cosy.

The relationship between Harry and Kim was quietly blossoming. It had been clear from the start that there was a mutual attraction, but until the rescue, this hadn't progressed beyond the occasional snatched conversation. Since their return, any reservations they might have had about his "royal" status seemed to have been forgotten. They were constantly together and the happiness that radiated from them was enough to lift the darkest mood on those bleak winter days.

The only expeditions we embarked on were to check on the welfare of the groups closest to us.

We were only too aware that they didn't have the luxury of a large quantity of stored supplies to fall back on as we did, and we knew that they would be finding it just as difficult to navigate the snow-filled streets and roads.

Their food levels would be running low by now, due to the difficulties of scavenging effectively.

Teams of volunteers, heavily laden with rucksacks full of supplies, set out to see them, and returned exhausted many hours later, with stories of the appalling conditions out there and with messages of thanks from grateful communities.

All the groups were given assurances that, as they'd agreed to follow the plan and been promised a place at the base, help would be made available to them until the plan could be put into action.

Jerry finally declared me fit for duty, but to my frustration, there was very little that I could do.

Pete was constantly thinking up ways to keep people busy: organising games and competitions, and persuading anyone with an area of expertise to give a lecture.

Allan, who with the help of the engineers, was always desperate to start on another project, constructed a firing range on a neighbouring street and set about training us all on how to use the new weapons we'd received from the base. The "range hut", heated by a rudimentary fireplace, provided much needed shelter for his eager pupils while they waited their turn, and soon everyone had a basic level of competence on all the new weapons we had.

We talked about our own way of life now and how it compared to that of the early pioneers and people living subsistence lifestyles. Like them, we'd spent the warmer months gathering enough food and supplies to last us through the long winter and now, forced by the weather, we were having to spend long periods of time cooped up together.

We kept "cabin fever" at bay by occupying ourselves with jobs or just enjoying the opportunity to spend time together and strengthen our family and friendship bonds.

It must have been incredibly hard on the smaller groups. We at least had the knowledge that the weather would only last for a few more weeks to keep us going, but the size of our community was also a huge benefit, as there was always someone different to interact with, and a new and different conversation or activity to join in with. But still, with every new fall of snow we would ask ourselves, "How much longer will this go on for?" The weather was never far from anyone's mind.

As January slowly turned into February, the weather began to improve and temperatures rose slightly. Although snowdrifts up to a couple of metres deep still lay against the walls of the houses, we began to hope for a thaw. From the lookout post we'd constructed at the top of the church tower, we'd spotted a few distant plumes of smoke, possibly a sign of other groups we hadn't discovered yet.

Using a mixture of compass bearings, maps and local knowledge, we managed to identify their approximate positions in the hope of paying them a visit once conditions allowed.

Eventually the snow levels dropped enough to attempt to reach the base by vehicle. As we had nothing better to do, we all gathered round to watch as the two armoured vehicles left the compound, their crew compartments full of soldiers.

There hadn't been sufficient room for everyone who'd been scheduled to return, but although many of them had young families they were desperate to see back at the base, no one had wanted to take someone else's place.

So, when volunteers were called for, not one of them had applied. It finally came down to Harry picking names out of a helmet, refusing to take no for an answer and ordering the lucky winners to "just get on the bloody bus!"

As we huddled together shivering in the near-zero temperatures, watching the vehicles until they disappeared around the corner, my eyes were naturally drawn to the tracks left in the snow.

Absentmindedly, I remarked to Allan, who was standing beside me, "If we don't get another fall of snow, until that lot melts we'll have a bloody great arrow advertising where we are and where the base is."

Allan nodded thoughtfully, "Well there's not much we can do about that now. But with the measures we've already taken and the new weapons and extra manpower we have, I'm pretty sure we can keep ourselves safe. Things will only go wrong if we relax or drop our guard."

We turned and walked back into the house.

CHAPTER FIVE

As we watched the snow gradually retreat, we began to look forward to venturing out again and wondered what the coming year would bring. We were confident that we could protect ourselves against physical threats and we still had the reassurance of a store of food for back-up, and the skills and knowledge to catch or grow more, so we weren't too concerned about going hungry.

Yes, we knew there were still dangers out there, but we felt in no immediate peril.

As I'd predicted, groups and individuals had begun to appear at the barricades. They were all in a pitiful state and weak from starvation, malnutrition and frostbite. Out of sheer pity we offered them whatever help we could, but we couldn't afford to allow them inside the compound. We prepared more houses outside for them to stay in and recuperate, and offered them all the medical help and food they needed, but after the last incident, we'd had to harden our hearts and stick to what we'd agreed.

We weren't going to place anyone from the community in danger out of a misguided sense of kindness and trust.

Although we found it hard to believe, their stories made it clear that they were the lucky ones. They had survived. Thousands more had been unable to find food, and had either starved to death or been preyed upon by gangs who'd stolen everything they'd managed to gather. Most had been discouraged from returning to the cities by the alarming accounts given by the people who were escaping. Instead, they'd opted for trying to survive in the countryside. Many of them had banded together for protection, working together to gather what food was available.

The human body is capable of withstanding the most extraordinary hardship. If the stories they told applied to the rest of the country, then clearly millions of people had been clinging to survival by their very fingernails.

But then the winter had hit and many had lost their battle with the freezing temperatures. Whole families had huddled together under blankets in whatever shelter they could find, and died. The conditions had made it impossible to venture out. As soon as they were able to, the few that remained had been forced to leave behind the bodies of their family members and friends. The few who managed to reach us said that even the route to us, through the tyre tracks, had been littered with the bodies of people who had almost made it.

The base was reporting similar stories. Due to a shortage of suitable accommodation they were building a tented village to house the survivors.

We knew that what we were doing was important to the recovery programme.

If we could play just a small part in nursing these people back to health, then hopefully they would be strong enough to travel to the base to begin the important work of growing food for everyone, safe in the knowledge that they and their families would be under the protection of the base.

Towards the end of February, the weather changed abruptly. The temperature rose by fifteen degrees and we experienced a bewildering mixture of clear sunny days, interchanged with days of torrential rain. The melting snow and the heavy rain caused widespread local flooding. As there are no major rivers or waterways flowing through Birmingham, we escaped the worst of it, with just a few roads rendered impassable by a swollen stream or brook. We knew the waters would soon subside.

By this time, every last trace of the snow had gone, and along with it, the tracks that had led the refugees to our door.

The smoke from our cooking fires was still a beacon of hope for the few who managed to make it to us or one of our neighbours, but there were far fewer now, and most of these were escorted by the other communities around us.

Including the people who had approached the base, a quick census revealed that we'd still only been able to save two hundred and fifty people. And now that the snows had gone, patrols sent out from the base came back with shocking reports of fields choked with the dead bodies of men, women and children. The planners set themselves the grim task of re-calculating the expected survival rate.

It came out at a truly shocking five percent.

According to their estimates, only three million people were left alive in the United Kingdom (about half the population of the West Midlands, prior to the event). We shook our heads in despair. We'd seen so few people lately, we knew it was entirely possible that the number was even lower than that.

Weekly convoys began between our road and the base, primarily to transport the new arrivals, who wanted to take part in the recovery plan. Most were keen to participate, having recognised that it was the only way to ensure their survival, but inexplicably, one or two still refused.

While they were recovering, we offered them support, but if they were declared fit enough to travel and then showed no interest in the recovery plan, we lost no time in giving them a quantity of supplies, wishing them well and sending them on their way. If they weren't prepared to contribute, then they could expect no more help from us.

The missions to secure the weapon locations were mainly successful. Large quantities of weapons had been recovered and although a few places were found to be empty, with signs of forced entry, the majority were still secure.

The "gun culture" had never been prevalent in British society, so we assumed that most people had concentrated primarily on food rather than worrying about weapons.

Few people would have known where to find firearms and even fewer would have known how to use them. It was easy to see how so many people could have fallen prey to gangs like Gumin's.

As the convoys spread out across the country, they kept us informed of the survivors they found. The people they encountered were given the following options:

They could remain where they were, sign up to the recovery plan and wait to be contacted again once the plan could be coordinated on a national level.

They could head directly to the base in Herefordshire, and depending on the skills they had, they could begin to contribute to the plan there.

If they were likely to pass by us on the way to the base, they were given our location and asked to wait for a "lift" on the next convoy. If this was the case, we were informed of the size of their group and given an approximate arrival date, so that we could prepare for them.

A few of the groups we were notified about never arrived, and some reported attacks from other communities or roving gangs. For the ones who hadn't arrived, we could only assume the worst.

If we were given enough information to pinpoint the locations of a gang or a hostile community, Paul Berry would set out with some heavily armed men on a "search and destroy" mission. In some cases, after some careful handling, amicable relations were established after all, and the targets would willingly sign up to the plan. Other groups had clearly been attacked too many times and lost too many people. They were no longer prepared to trust anyone and adopted a "shoot first, ask questions later" policy. Sadly, this left the mission commander with no room for negotiation and he would have to use whatever force was necessary to eliminate them.

CHAPTER SIX

Although much of our time was now taken up with helping the survivors that approached us, we still had a community to run, and as a matter of pride we were keen to continue scavenging, hunting and growing our own food rather than just relying on the stores we had.

We began to sow and tend to the areas that we had already prepared, and worked hard to clear more ground. More areas were being cultivated, because we were planning to create an extensive area of polytunnels to enable us to grow food all year round.

The chickens and rabbits were proving very successful. Butch had lived up to his name and had already sired his first litter. We planned to let the population grow a little before using them for food but as we all knew it was likely to explode shortly, we were looking forward to the prospect of rabbit stew on the menu.

McQueen the rooster was enjoying himself to such an extent we'd had to expand the chicken run with a separate nursery area to accommodate the new arrivals.

The farmer at the base was providing us with a wealth of information and advice on how we could make the best use of what we had available. The radio calls to the base sometimes sounded like episodes of Farmer's Question Time.

Chris Garland was running continuous Forest Skills courses and educating us all in bushcraft, survival and foraging skills. He taught us that nature surrounds us with all sorts of things that can be put to good use, or be a valuable source of nutrition. In fact, his lessons were proving so popular that Pete was obliged to make up a waiting list so that everyone would have an opportunity to learn.

As Chris explained, you never stopped learning, because each new season yielded new treasures, many of them edible, and useful additions to our food stocks.

We continued with the foraging missions, although the radius of these was expanding continually as we systematically stripped out anything we could use from houses, offices, shops and warehouses.

These missions also functioned as security patrols, and enabled us to keep in touch with the few groups that had decided to remain and help with the recovery plan by becoming as self-sufficient as possible. They in turn, would then be in a position to offer help to anyone who approached them.

We set up a rudimentary trading scheme with these groups, exchanging surplus goods or passing on requests or messages from other groups living beyond the range of their territory. We also delivered seeds and medical supplies from the government stores.

If they were participating in the plan, then the government was determined to offer what assistance it could, however small that might be, as a sign that they were receiving their support. The trades were rarely to our advantage, but we knew that we were setting an important precedent.

We also offered a meal and a drink to any passing foraging patrol from other communities we knew. And if it was getting too late for them to return, we also gave them a bed for the night.

The other groups began to reciprocate, and this helped to strengthen the bonds between us.

As we'd hoped, tracking down the distant smoke trails seen from the church tower, had brought to light a few new groups and we'd succeeded in making contact. Most decided to head for Herefordshire but a few still opted to remain.

The government policy change that had resulted from the women's abduction made sense to us all. We agreed that it had been the right thing to do.

The plan had been for most people to leave the base and begin working mainly on agricultural projects. As the population increased, so did the need for additional space. No one new was being allowed access to the base facilities. They would be told about it, but as all they required was shelter and food, these could be provided above ground. Therefore, there was really no need for them to enter the base.

Occasionally an exception might be made for someone with a specific skill, or for a medical emergency, for which the base hospital might be required.

In the future, as the number of its occupants dwindled, the plan was for the base to become an administration hub. Possibly, I was told, it might be "mothballed" altogether at some point, as by then it would probably just be a waste of valuable resources.

As the weeks wore on, a new problem presented itself, which threatened to seriously undermine everything we'd achieved.

From the outset, we'd been careful to burn the bodies of our enemies, mindful that from a "public health" perspective, this was the best way of disposing of them. We'd also adopted this policy with any bodies we found in the locality. But now that the snow had gone and we were venturing further out, we discovered that the bodies of thousands of people lay rotting where they had died. Horrified, we set about the grisly business of trying to dispose of them.

But the sheer volume of bodies made this task impossible, and as the temperatures rose higher, we quickly began to realise that our efforts weren't making the slightest dent in the number that were still decomposing in the sun.

The receding floodwaters, which had affected the entire country, had other unexpected and terrible results.

The River Rea, a small river that flows through Birmingham, had been transformed into a raging torrent by the meltwater and heavy rain, before subsiding and becoming a gentle stream again.

But as a result, the bodies of hundreds of men, women and children lay discarded like litter along its length, either trapped by obstacles in the flowing water, or thrown up on to the banks on either side. They must have been washed into the river by the floods. The River Rea is just a short tributary of the River Tame, and only fifteen miles long. I could only imagine what all the other riverbanks in the country looked like.

Like everyone else, I found it impossible to look down on such an apocalyptic scene for more than a few seconds. Yet I knew with sickening certainty that the image of it would stay with me forever.

The sun shone down without pity, the increasing warmth accelerating the rate of decay. Some of the bodies were in a more advanced state of decomposition than others, suggesting that they had met their deaths before the freeze had begun. Clouds of flies swarmed over and around the bodies and carrion birds pecked and pulled mercilessly at the rotting flesh. Every time a patrol passed one of these scenes, played out along the river, they brought back reports of the worsening stench and the growing number of rats and dogs that could be seen feeding on the pitiful remains.

Before long the sweet, cloying smell of death and decay was making its way as far as our community. Depending on the wind direction, it varied from being faintly unpleasant to stomach churning.

Either way, we had no choice but to endure it and hope that time would bring it to a natural conclusion.

Understandably, the reek from the bodies had a terrible effect on morale. Moods darkened and tempers became frayed, as the miasma of evil settled over the whole community.

CHAPTER SEVEN

Dogs, up until now, had not been much of a problem, but now we began to see them more frequently.

Out of all of us, the few dogs we kept as pets on the road, including my two, had adapted best to life after the event. They'd readily accepted the increasing size of their "packs" as neighbours moved in with each other, presumably because this meant more fuss and attention. When the fences had first come down between the properties, there had been a few minor tiffs between them, while the hierarchy in the four-legged community was established, but that soon settled down.

Most dogs gradually assumed the role of family protector, as if they were aware that everyone had a part to play in the community. When not begging for food in the kitchen area, they could constantly be found mooching around the compound and sometimes further afield, seemingly on the lookout for intruders.

Their barking often gave us advanced warning of visitors before we were even aware of their presence.

As soon as one of our dogs began to bark everyone would be on the alert, in case someone hostile was approaching. For that reason alone, not once had anyone moaned about the food they ate. They played an important part in keeping us all safe.

If anything, there had been a notable absence of other dogs since the event, and we presumed that most had left the city with their owners or, if abandoned, had followed the mass exodus of people fleeing the city in search of food and safety. It was also entirely possible that as the food situation worsened and starvation took hold, dogs might have been on the menu.

But now packs of dogs were often seen roaming the neighbourhood. Although they didn't appear to be dangerous, they'd shaken off any last vestiges of domesticity and shied away from human contact.

There was rarely any conflict between the different packs but this, we soon realised, was a result of full bellies. There was no reason to fight over food when there were ample corpses lying around. Once we'd realised this, we began to view them rather differently.

We didn't want our own domesticated dogs mixing with these packs, as we weren't at all sure how they'd fare with their feral counterparts, so we were careful not to let them escape. Following the event, and in the absence of cars that might endanger them, they'd been able to come and go as they pleased. Now, to their obvious disgust, they found themselves being kept on leads, or only being given their freedom in areas we knew they couldn't escape from. The fact that this enforced incarceration was for their own good was lost on them, and there was much howling and whining in protest.

The first sign of trouble came soon enough. A scavenging patrol reported being silently followed by a large pack of dogs.

They hadn't felt threatened by them exactly, but the experience had been strange enough for them to report it. Before long, we realised that the rotting remains were rapidly being reduced to piles of bones.

Now that food was becoming scarce for them, were they sizing us up as an alternative?

The next few days brought more worrying reports. The dogs were becoming less timid now and were coming closer to the patrols, only retreating when scared off by a shout or a thrown object.

People were beginning to feel uneasy, as the dogs never moved far, just out of throwing range, and their eyes were constantly on them.

Another ominous development in the short history of our little community. Then one day, matters finally came to a head.

I was lost in my thoughts on guard duty, when I realised that my dog, who had been keeping me company, was making a low growling noise in his throat.

Gradually, the growling intensified and turned into frantic barking, at which point the other dogs in the community began to join in. Seconds later, twenty or so dogs trotted into view. They were thin, in poor condition and completely silent.

With a look of quiet intent on their faces, they began to make their way warily towards the barrier. I shouted, grabbed a stone and threw it in their general direction, fully expecting them to scatter and run. The stone rebounded off the road, inches from the pack leader but instead of running they stopped, looked back at me in a way that sent shivers down my spine, and then continued to creep closer, becoming bolder with every step.

By this time the noise from our own dogs was deafening, and people were running out of the houses to see what was happening.

"Grab her!" shouted someone, and I turned hurriedly to look. Jessie, a Border Collie, who had been adopted after being abandoned by a departing family, was making her way towards me.

Deftly avoiding outstretched arms and barking furiously, with hackles raised, she streaked past me and flung herself at the barrier. Before any of us could reach her, she'd climbed nimbly up and over the wall of tonne sacks before crawling through the gap beneath the gates.

We watched in horror as the approaching pack noted her arrival and began baring their teeth and snarling. Undaunted, Jessie stood before them, barking and snapping, warning them furiously to stay away in a desperate attempt to protect us, and oblivious to the danger she was in.

The growing crowd behind me watched in suspense as the drama unfolded and then I realised with a jolt that the snarling pack were beginning to surround the collie, closing in on her. Without thinking, I raised my weapon, sighted it carefully on the most aggressive looking dog, and pulled the trigger.

In hindsight, it would have been better to use an unsilenced weapon, as the noise would have acted as a deterrent to the other dogs. Instead, my gun emitted a few low cracks and the pack leader was knocked over. It yelped in pain, thrashed its legs for a few seconds, and lay still.

I'd killed the first dog instinctively, but aiming my weapon a second time, as the other dogs began to run around in confusion, was somehow much harder than it had been when human beings were attacking us. Those people had chosen to try to kill us and therefore it was easier to justify your own response. Using guns to hunt animals to put food on the table was also completely different.

Shooting a dog that had once been someone's pet was much harder. But Jessie was out there risking her life for us, so I pushed any sentimental feelings aside.

As the others raised their weapons, Jessie, as if sensing that her work was done, managed to break through and get back to us.

The remaining dogs gave chase, but she was too quick for them. She squeezed under the gate and scrambled up and over the tonne sack wall several metres ahead of her pursuers.

When I'd killed the first dog, I'd expected them to scatter and run but I was shocked to find that they only renewed their assault, crawling under the gate, and scrabbling furiously to get over the inner wall. We were a threat to them and their intent was clear; they wanted to tear us apart. And they'd acquired a taste for human flesh.

Before we had time to react, a huge German Shepherd flung itself up and over the barrier and went for a soldier's throat. Knocking him backwards, it sank its teeth into the arm he'd instinctively raised to defend himself. Unable to fire directly at it, in case they hit the screaming soldier, everyone close by began frantically clubbing the dog with their weapons. This only seemed to enrage the dog, and it tightened its grip. Amidst the chaos, I realised that more dogs were still trying to climb the wall.

Harry's shouted command of "Fire!" snapped us all out of it and we began shooting at the seething mass of barking, snapping and snarling animals. One minute and a few magazine changes later, they were all lying dead or mortally wounded, whining and yelping as their life blood drained away.

Chris Garland stood over the German Shepherd with his knife in his hands, blood dripping from the end of the blade. He'd had to resort to stabbing the dog repeatedly to get it to release its hold on the soldier.

Apart from the groans from the bitten man, the rest of us stood around in silence, shocked at the events of the past few minutes.

I wiped the sweat out of my eyes and remarked, "Well that escalated quickly!"

The soldier was quickly taken off to have his arm looked at by Jerry. Despite our fears, it didn't look too bad, because his thick jacket had served as some protection, but he still had some nasty puncture wounds which would need to be cleaned to stop them becoming infected.

All work ground to a halt while we gathered together to discuss what had happened.

A few people expressed fears that we were going to be besieged by packs of killer dogs, but eventually we all agreed that yes, for the immediate future, the dogs were likely to be a problem and therefore we would need to be very careful. As a sensible precaution, we would adopt the strategy of "safety in numbers".

But hopefully, the crisis would pass once the food supply from the dead was exhausted, and the packs dispersed in search of easier pickings. We also hoped that their numbers would begin to drop as hunger set in and natural selection asserted itself, with the stronger dogs weeding out the weaker ones to ensure that they had enough to eat.

In fact, I thought wryly, the weaker ones among them would probably be their next meal.

Pete quickly organised a work party to dispose of the dogs' carcasses.

Within an hour, the rising plume of smoke from their funeral pyre marked the passing of another eventful day. Most of the working party complained that they'd been virtually eaten alive by fleas from the dogs, and scratched at the irritating bites around the exposed skin of their wrists and necks for some hours afterwards.

CHAPTER EIGHT

A day or two later, I was on early morning guard duty, patrolling the perimeter fence and watching the sun rise in the eastern sky. It looked as if it was going to be a fine day. Suddenly the silence was broken by shouts of dismay and annoyance from the garden area I'd been making for. I picked up my pace to investigate.

Russ's wife, Jo and Mary were running up towards the houses, so I called out to them.

"What is it? What's the matter?"

"Bloody rats are eating everything!" shouted Jo, a look of disgust on her face. They came to a halt and waited for me to catch up with them. "There must be thousands of them!" she panted.

"We went to let the chickens out and see if there were any eggs for breakfast. Since most of them have had their first chicks, they've hardly been laying any, but now the chicks are starting to look after themselves we were hoping to start getting the odd one or two.

Anyway, that's irrelevant now, because the chicken run's overrun with rats and most of the small chicks have disappeared."

I made my way hastily towards the chicken coop with Jo and Mary following close behind.

It was true. The coop and the area around it was literally crawling with squirming rats.

The chickens were perched anywhere they could find to get away from them and were squawking and clucking loudly in protest. The rats were jumping over each other to get at them and the chickens were flapping their wings in alarm and pecking at them as soon as they came anywhere near them.

I turned to Jo. "Go and get some help while I try to get the chickens out of there." Handing Mary my gun to hold, I picked up a broom that was leaning up against the mesh side of the coop. Swallowing my disgust at the sight of the tangle of seething bodies, I opened the door to the coop and began knocking them out of the way with the broom.

The chickens and McQueen had spotted my approach and their volume increased, as if they knew that help was at hand. As soon as I opened the door, they all flapped past me and made their way comically up the garden and away from the rats, squawking indignantly as they went.

A quick look round convinced me that none of the chicks had survived, so I backed out of the chicken run, angrily swiping at the rats to clear a path. I felt a great sense of satisfaction when the broom head made contact with one, hurling it into the side of the coop and killing it stone dead, but watched, sickened, as the other rats immediately pounced on it and began ripping it apart.

More people were arriving now to see what the commotion was about, and we all looked on helplessly as the rats scurried here and there, devouring everything in their path. Even the vegetables we had planted, which had been pushing up green shoots, had been nibbled away to nothing and destroyed.

We tried everything we could think of to scare them away, but they just moved en masse to another place and carried on voraciously feeding. Every able-bodied man, woman and child was mustered, and armed with anything we could find that might kill them or scare them away, but in the end, there were just too many of them. After an hour of frantic smashing and bashing we were all exhausted. It had been a futile exercise and we were forced to call a halt to it.

We had no idea what to do. No one had experienced anything like this before. Pete shouted to everyone that a meeting would be held in the kitchen area to discuss the next step, and we all began to make our way there.

As we walked into the kitchen, it became clear that things were getting worse.

Rats were running in all directions. They'd entered the houses unnoticed when everyone had gone outside to help. Panic struck me. "The food!" I screamed. "They'll eat the lot!"

Quickly, Pete ordered everyone who was present to head either to the kitchen area or to the main food store, which was in his house. He then ran off to raise the alarm with everyone else. Allan, Jerry and I, followed by a few others, made straight for my basement and garage area.

Although there were a few rats skittering about, to my immense relief they hadn't managed to get into my garage storeroom and they hadn't yet discovered the basement room, where we kept the rest of our supplies. Silently patting myself on the back for doing such a good job of building it in the first place, I began to look for all the places they might be able to get in through, with a view to blocking these up.

As only a few of us were needed for this task, I sent everyone else to find Pete and see if they could help elsewhere.

Pete was in a much worse predicament. The rats had been all over the supplies in his house and the place was a mess.

Thinking quickly, he organised a chain of people to empty the rooms of any supplies that hadn't been chewed and spoiled. In the meantime, a second group worked furiously to kill and clear out as many rats as possible.

The military supplies had fared better, as most were stored in purpose-built sealed containers, so once the soldiers had secured the supplies they had in the compound, they mucked in with everyone else to help.

Finally, the supplies that they'd managed to salvage were stacked neatly on Pete's drive, protected by a determined ring of club-wielding residents and soldiers.

Satisfied that my own supplies were as safe as I could make them, I joined the others.

Now began the difficult process of clearing all the houses of the rodent invaders. Most of them were concentrated around any potential food sources, but we checked everywhere we could think, just in case they'd found somewhere else to use as a nest.

Every drawer, cupboard and hidey-hole was investigated. All the houses were turn of the century: Edwardian or Victorian, and not the modern, badly built sealed boxes of more recent times, so it was virtually impossible to keep them out. They were full of gaps and holes that provided ideal access points for rats.

It took many hours of painstaking work before we were satisfied that all the houses were as clear as we could make them. The odd rat could still be seen scurrying about, but we were satisfied that we'd done as much as we could.

Exhausted and grubby, we all gathered together again in the kitchen area. The whole cooking area had had to be scrubbed clean, but even now the cooks, who were trying to keep us all fuelled with drinks and food, needed constant protection to keep the rats away from the food they were handling.

If the situation hadn't been so serious it would have been comical.

I watched people running back and forth, waving whatever weapon came to hand, cursing the rat in question and shouting at it to show itself.

Realising that we couldn't possibly leave the food stacked on Pete's front drive, we wearily set about transferring it to my storage area. Once that was full, we used my trailer and wheelbarrows to transport them up the road and squeezed the rest into the container the soldiers had.

In the gathering gloom, everyone apart from the people on guard duty slumped down exhausted in the communal kitchen.

Pete called for silence and stood on a table so that everyone could see him.

"Thanks, everyone. You've all worked damn hard today. And if I may say so, this has been a heck of a day! I'm not sure what other challenges are going to be thrown at us, but once again this community has proved its worth. We've worked together and we've saved most of our supplies. I haven't managed to carry out a full inventory yet, but fortunately we got to them in time. All things considered, very little was damaged. And anything the rats did get into won't be wasted; we'll feed it to the animals.

The bad news is that all the chicks have gone, and we'll have to wait for daylight to assess the extent of the damage to our crops. But we can grow more crops and the chickens will continue to lay eggs."

He looked round at our tired, dirt-streaked faces. "We'll recover from this. It's just a small blip. Yes, we're tired and discouraged, but try not to worry. Hopefully, the rats won't be a problem for long. I've just had a long conversation with people back at the base, and they're in the same situation. There's been an unprecedented rise in the rat population due to a glut of food.

They've been feeding off the dead, just like the dogs. But it's important to bear in mind that as this food source diminishes, and it *is* starting to, so will the rat population.

We don't know how long that will take, but as most of the cadavers have been picked clean, they've moved on to us: the closest available food source. But if they can't get food from us they should, in theory, move on. We just need to be vigilant from now on. So, until this crisis has passed, all work apart from guard duty will be cancelled, and for want of a better phrase, we'll all be on 'rat patrol'."

He waited to see if anyone disagreed or had anything else to add, but by now most people were too tired to even think. Some people nodded but otherwise no one made any comment.

Pete nodded, satisfied, "Great. Thank you, all of you. I'll be round with a revised rota soon. I think it would be best for now if we all eat in our homes. It'll be easier to keep the rats away, and if there's less food outside it'll hopefully discourage them."

Tired as I was that night, I swear I could hear tiny scurrying feet everywhere.

It was very hard to get to sleep.

CHAPTER NINE

Over the following week, we kept fires burning continuously at various points around the compound so that we could dispose of the dead rats quickly and easily. If you didn't pick one up and throw it on to the nearest fire as soon as you'd killed it, it was soon eaten by another. And that would just keep them around for longer.

The packs of dogs had finally dispersed, the rats having proved to be a much easier source of food for them. We spotted the odd one or two chasing rats, but as we weren't leaving the compound much, we had other things to worry about.

The base in Herefordshire had been overrun as well, but they'd been able to protect most of the food they had stored. The crops in the fields and the polytunnels had been ruined, but plans were in progress to replant as soon as the rat population had diminished enough. Paul and I undertook a tour of the groups closest to us in an armoured car. The group at the food warehouse in Redditch had fared the best. As all their food was stored on racking, they'd been better able to protect it. One particularly inventive resident had fabricated a cone-shaped collar that prevented the rats from climbing the racking.

The others had been less fortunate. To a greater or lesser degree, they'd all been invaded by the rats and had lost most of their meagre supplies.

We distributed the supplies we'd brought with us, in the hope that these would keep them going.

For most of them, this had been the final straw. Although they'd hoped to remain independent, they just didn't feel that this was possible anymore. They announced their intention of heading for the base, where they would do all they could to aid the recovery from there.

Paul and I tried to talk them round and we did manage to persuade some of them to change their minds, but few could see a way past the difficulty of having lost most of the food they'd worked so hard to gather or grow. I can't say I blamed them.

After discussing the issue with Jerry's brother, Jon, we decided that the best course of action would be to use every vehicle we had and orchestrate one large convoy to transport everyone who wanted to return to the base in one go. We didn't have enough supplies to feed them all, and as some had virtually no food left at all, it would be best to start out as soon as possible.

Of course, that would leave us without any transport other than my Land Rover, but we decided that wouldn't matter. It would only be one or two days until the convoy returned.

The following day we re-visited the groups that wanted to go and instructed them to pack what they needed and wait for transport, which would be arriving the day after.

As we were planning to use all the vehicles and would therefore have sufficient space, we advised them to bring anything they thought would be useful as it was unlikely that they'd be able to return.

Once all the vehicles had left, the road seemed deserted. Most of the soldiers had also now gone and weren't due to be replaced until the convoy returned in a day or so. Paul and Harry, as always, had been reluctant to return home and once again had managed to find a reason not to go back to the base. Paul felt that his skills as an SAS Captain were needed here. Harry clearly didn't want to be too far from Kim.

Except for Paul, Harry and Chris, and two soldiers who'd elected to remain as they had no family back at the base, for the first time in months, only the original inhabitants of the road were left. To mark the occasion, Pete announced a day of rest.

We'd all been working furiously "rat-bashing" (this had had become something of a local sport) and putting everything back in order after the rat invasion, or the "chickapocalypse", as some of us were referring to it, given its catastrophic effect on our chick population.

Thankfully, the number of rats was diminishing day by day, although the ones that remained, presumably the "ninjas" of the rat race, seemed infuriatingly adept at evading capture.

The easiest way to kill them was from a distance, using an air rifle, and Stanley and the other children on the road had proved such good shots that they had taken the job over from the adults. Every day they would set themselves up at various positions around the compound and run a competition to see who got the biggest "bag" of the day.

It was typical of our community to use humour to get us through the tough times, and I was reminded of a story I'd heard from Paul about the terrible war in Afghanistan.

When the British and American forces had been attacking the heavily defended Tora Bora cave complex, they'd suffered horrendous casualties. The Americans had referred to them as: "Tora Bora: caves of death!" whereas the British had called them "Tora Bora Tomkinson", after the well-known socialite.

Our community now consisted of thirty-nine adults and fifteen children.

The children quickly dispersed for the day, either to play or to continue rat hunting, an activity they never seemed to tire of. In the meantime, Pete adjusted the guard rota so that it changed regularly, and no one was kept away for too long, then we all settled down to a day of relaxation and laughter.

Some hours later, I noticed Jerry looking thoughtfully at Jo. Since her husband had been killed at the barricade at the time of the kidnapping, she'd understandably been left heartbroken.

She'd always been quite a frail woman and her husband's death had left her very low. We were hopeful that time and the friendship we could offer her would help her to recover, and it had been nice to see her smile and join in with some of the conversations that were taking place in the kitchen.

"Jo, do you feel OK?" asked Jerry. "You look a bit hot and flushed."

Leaning forward, he felt her forehead.

He quickly withdrew his hand. "You're running a bit of a temperature. Have you had plenty of water today?"

Jo said she hadn't and that, yes, she was feeling a bit warm, but she would drink a few glasses of water, take a paracetamol and would soon feel better.

An hour later, she stood up, looking a little pale, and said she was still feeling a bit under the weather and would go for a lie down.

Jerry nodded and promised to pop in and check on her in half an hour.

She took two steps forward and fainted.

Jerry and the people closest to her ran forward to help, while the rest of us stood up uncertainly, in case we were needed. At Jerry's request, we all stood back to give him the space to examine her.

After a quick examination, I could see the concern growing on his face and he quickly began to check various parts of her body. Then he stood up abruptly, and took a step back.

"Stay back, everyone!"

Turning to Fiona, he said urgently, "Go and get my bag, and bring the box of gloves and masks with you, please." Without asking questions, Fiona sped off.

He turned to the rest of us and said, "I need to examine her further and I don't want to frighten anyone, but unless I'm mistaken, she has some sort of virus. Don't worry, she'll be OK, but until we know what it is, I think it's best if you all keep your distance."

I looked at him carefully. He was worried but he wasn't giving anything away.

He asked me to fetch the wheeled stretcher we'd acquired on one of our scavenging trips. Then donning masks and gloves, some of us helped him take her into his "surgery".

Jo's illness had cast a shadow over the day. As we waited anxiously for news, the children piled in, looking hot and bothered after their games. Two of them, Laura and Ben, approached their mother.

"Mummy," said Laura, her face puckering up as she started to cry, "I don't feel very well." As she sat them both down Ben, who'd been uncharacteristically quiet, vomited and passed out.

Everyone took an involuntary step backwards. Three people falling ill and fainting in such a short space of time. Something was going on.

As someone ran off to fetch Jerry, we stood in silence, exchanging nervous glances.

CHAPTER TEN

"They've got the bubonic plague. I'm absolutely certain. The symptoms are easily identifiable."

Silence. We all stared at him in shock. The bubonic plague: The Black Death. We weren't in medieval England! Nobody caught the Black Death anymore.

Jerry, looking pale and grim, continued.

"Yes, it still exists. Admittedly most modern cases have been in Africa, but given the right circumstances it could easily occur here." Shaking his head, he added, "I blame myself. I should have insisted on better precautions as soon as the rats appeared."

"Why?" asked Becky.

"Fleas, Becky. The fleas on the rats carry the bacteria. The fleas bite us and the infection spreads."

"What's the treatment, Doc?" asked Harry.

"Antibiotics, basically. Hopefully what I've given Jo, Ben and Laura will work. My one concern is that even though I'm certain of my diagnosis, the timescale wasn't what I'd expect. Admittedly, I've never treated someone with this before, but I've looked it all up and it seems to be affecting them differently. I'm worried we may be facing a new strain of the disease.

In light of this, I'm recommending that we immediately start operating under quarantine conditions. We'll need to separate ourselves off from each other as much as possible to try to limit the spread. We don't know who's already infected; we could all be. Only time will tell."

We all looked at each other, fear making us dumb.

"If you could all individually collect a mask and surgical gloves from the boxes I have here and go back to your house, we'll work out the finer details later. As soon as anyone feels the slightest bit ill, you must tell me. The sooner the antibiotics are given, the better the chance you'll have."

I spoke up, "Jerry, we all know from history that the Black Death killed off about half the population of Europe. How good is this treatment? You don't sound certain."

He shrugged, "Truthfully, I don't know. I know without treatment the death rate is about eighty percent. With antibiotics, the survival rate is usually quite good, but as I said, this isn't following the usual pattern. I can't be certain, but I don't have a good feeling about this.

The rats have been feasting on rotting human flesh for weeks. Bacteria can mutate and adapt to the environment they're in. My concern is that we may be dealing with something new. Without a full laboratory test, we won't be able to tell.

Now please, go back to your houses and keep a careful eye on each other. If anyone falls ill, I'll do everything I can to help. But to be honest, treatment is simple: antibiotics, fluids and general care. And we can all do that.

If this spreads, I could get it as well, so I'll prepare as many doses of antibiotics as I can and leave detailed care instructions so that you'll be able to look after each other."

Turning silently, and clutching our children close, our household made its way back home.

We gathered in the kitchen, still masked, and gazed helplessly at each other.

"What shall we do?" asked Jane, breaking the silence.

A scurrying noise made us all turn, and we watched miserably as a rat ran across the kitchen floor and disappeared through the open back door.

"I don't think we can hide from this," I said. "We'll just have to hope that the precautions we have in place now will be enough. If we already have it, we won't be able to do much about it. And if Laura, Ben and Jo have it, the chances are that someone else will have it too. Most likely, they're standing in this room."

We all peered at each other, as if careful scrutiny might be sufficient to force the hidden organism to reveal itself.

I began again, "I think we should exercise extreme caution. Why don't we all grab some food and drink and retreat to our rooms for the next twenty-four hours or so? There's no point in trying to be a hero. Keep your masks on. If you have it, you won't want to spread it to the rest of your family, and if a member of your family has it, they'll need you to stay well so that you can look after them."

With a few "good lucks" and "God bless yous", we all shut ourselves in our rooms. After an hour in one room, struggling to entertain the children, it hit me that we were now more isolated than at any other time in our community's history.

Communication between the families was limited to shouting through closed doors to each other and we had no idea what was happening in the other houses. We also had no idea who, if anyone, was on guard duty.

The whole situation had arisen so suddenly that we'd had no time to put any measures in place. All we could do was follow Jerry's directions.

Only now, after contemplating the matter for an hour or two, did it occur to me that there could well be other serious consequences from the outbreak.

"Becky," I said, coming to a decision, "I need to go and sort a few things out." At the look on her face, I hastily added, "Don't worry, I won't go near anyone."

Before she could argue, I gave the kids a quick hug and headed out.

Before leaving the house, I checked through everyone's door to see if they were OK, explained that I was going out for a while, and asked if they needed anything.

Outside, the road was silent and deserted. It was the strangest feeling. At most times of the day or night there was always someone out and about. To find the road empty was an unsettling experience. Now it looked like all the other abandoned roads in the city.

Shrugging off my feelings of unease, I hurried over to Pete's house and called to him from his doorstep.

As he opened the door, I stepped back. By unspoken agreement we both felt more comfortable with six feet between us.

"Is everything OK at yours?" he asked anxiously. "I think Allan might have it; he's trying to get Michelle to leave him alone, but she won't hear of it. Jerry's been round and given him a dose of antibiotics, so fingers crossed we caught it in time."

I felt despair. Hard to believe that Allan, who had always been so strong and dependable, could have succumbed to the infection. In some ways, you could understand it with children and older folk because they were much more susceptible. But if Allan had caught it, then so could any one of us.

I dragged my thoughts back to the reason I was there in the first place.

"Pete, I've just realised there's no one on guard duty. We were all knocked off balance by Jerry's diagnosis, and we just blindly did what he told us. But we can't leave ourselves undefended, no matter what's happening. We're just asking for trouble."

I watched as a look of dawning comprehension crept over Pete's face, swiftly replaced by a look of embarrassment. To think that he, of all people, could have been caught out! The poor man was so mortified that I smiled in spite of myself.

"Pete, don't blame yourself. None of us remembered, and you've had other things on your mind. You've got a sick friend in your house. I only thought about it when I was sitting in my bedroom trying to think up something to do."

Pete nodded, somewhat mollified by my words. He now had that familiar look on his face; the one he always wore when he was planning. A noise from further up the road made us look round.

Harry, Paul, Chris and the two other soldiers were approaching, their faces half hidden by full face gas masks and all wearing surgical gloves.

Harry spoke, his voice oddly muffled, but sounding slightly sheepish all the same. "They might look like overkill, but they're infinitely better at keeping things out than those face masks you've got. In fact, they're horrible to wear for any amount of time, but we've got them so we may as well use them.

I've managed to scrounge up ten more sets. I think it would be best to give them to the people who are more likely to have had contact with the infected."

He placed a bag on the floor between us. "We've also realised that in all the fuss, no one's been watching the perimeter!"

Pete interrupted. "Yes, that's why Tom came to see me. Thanks for the gas masks, if that's what you call them now. Jerry and Fiona will need them and I'll allocate the others as necessary."

"I've had a think and I'll work out a rota for guard duty, taking into account the need to contain the spread of the disease …"

I grinned. Pete was back in action.

Paul stopped him by raising his hand. "They're actually called respirators, but gas masks works just as well. Don't worry, Pete, we've already talked things through and the five of us can manage the security situation. The rest of you have friends and family to worry about. We don't."

Paul caught the look I gave him. "OK, Tom. Friends yes, family no. But for the next couple of days, let us take care of things."

Pete shook his head. "It's too much to ask," he said. "It's very kind of you, but five of you can't cover everything."

"Yes, we can," said Harry firmly. "With the exception of Chris, we're all soldiers. A couple of days on reduced sleep is nothing we haven't done before. And if we need more help, we can raise the alarm using the normal procedures and you can all come running! Don't worry, we can do it. Anyway, we insist, so that's the end of it."

He paused and you could tell he was smiling behind his mask. "Don't make me get all 'royal' on you guys. You can still be hanged for disobeying a direct order from a monarch, I believe."

I laughed. "Oi, Prince Boy. You ain't my monarch…yet!"

He snorted inside his mask. "I can always get Grandmama on the radio if you like."

I held up my hands in mock surrender. "OK, OK, I agree. Thank you, thank you all. Pete, they're making sense to me. We can always be on hand in case they need us. Let's go back home."

Pete nodded and added his thanks. As I walked home, he called after me that he would get the gas masks to the right people.

CHAPTER ELEVEN

I was woken up the following morning by Jerry banging on my bedroom door and calling my name.

Realising that something must be wrong, I hastily scrambled out of bed and yanked the door open. The sight of Jerry in a full-face gas mask gave me quite a start. He looked like something out of a horror movie.

"I need a word with you outside. Now," he said quietly, and made his way back down the stairs. Having recovered from my shock, I threw some clothes on and followed him down.

He stood in the middle of the deserted kitchen area, careful to stay six feet away from me, removed his mask and took in a deep breath of fresh air. The anguish on his face made my heart sink.

"Jo and Laura died last night and we lost Ben twenty minutes ago."

His eyes filled with tears.

"There was nothing I could do; the antibiotics just didn't kick in quickly enough. I haven't seen or heard of anything this aggressive. They didn't stand a chance."

The words felt like a physical blow. I stood there for a moment looking at him, then instinctively took a step towards him, wanting to comfort him. He recoiled and took a step back.

"Don't, Tom," he said, wiping his eyes, "you need to keep your distance. I've been in extremely close contact with them. And the way this is spreading, it has to be highly contagious."

My heart sank even more. "Why? How many more are infected?"

"Allan was the next person to pick it up, but for some reason he's responding better to the antibiotics …" He paused, "or he's as strong and stubborn as an ox, and naturally resistant to diseases and it's nothing to do with me. Ten more people are also showing symptoms now," he added, reeling off their names, "but they're not doing so well. I'm not sure if any of them will make it."

I began to say something but he held up his hands. "Tom, just listen to me. There's no time to waste. I need you to look after my children for me. Everyone who isn't sick must leave immediately. In my opinion, it's the only way to avoid infection. Just look around you, for God's sake! The place is still crawling with rats and once someone has it they're highly infectious."

Dumbfounded, I asked without thinking, "Where shall we go?"

He looked at me and it struck me that he seemed to have aged years overnight. "Oh, for pity's sake, Tom. Anywhere but here! You work it out. Fiona and I will stay here and do what we can for the sick.

If we're careful about using the masks and we protect ourselves from flea bites, we should, in theory, be safe enough."

Paul must have seen us talking and came and joined us. Jerry quickly updated him on the deaths and the newly infected. I watched as he quickly took in what Jerry was saying and remained silent for a minute, thinking it over.

"Well Jerry, I think that's a brave decision and I think it's the right thing to do. We'll do everything we can to help." Briskly, he turned to me,

"Tom, I'll organise this. When it comes to mobilising quickly we've been trained to do it. We'll have to use your Land Rover and trailer, so could you get those ready please? I'll need Pete as well. He's got all the inventory lists.

Tom, find another adult on the way to getting your car, and send them to me. If we pull together we can be gone in a few hours. Will that be quick enough Jerry?"

Jerry nodded, "As far as I'm concerned, you should really leave now, but a few hours won't make much difference, given the measures we've taken. For anyone already infected, there's not much we can do for them. We just need to get as many people away from the vermin as we can. They're the reason the plague is here."

I hurried back to the house and summoned everyone from their rooms, asking them to meet me in the kitchen.

Five minutes later Michael was on his way to Paul with all the children who were old enough to help, and the women were packing rucksacks for each family with a few changes of clothing and other essential items.

Although my Land Rover hadn't been used since the rescue mission, we'd been careful to maintain it so that it would be ready to use at a moment's notice. Up until now it had proved invaluable so we'd taken the precaution of using a solar trickle charger to keep the battery topped up and routinely starting it up and running it for half an hour every week. This had clearly paid off. After disconnecting the trickle charger, it started without hesitation.

I pulled it forward, manhandled the trailer on to the tow bar, and after winding my garage door up, drove out on to the road.

Paul was still deep in discussion with Harry and Pete, surrounded by a crowd of adults and children. The two soldiers looked decidedly eerie in their masks.

Paul beckoned me over. "Right," he said briskly, "we've drawn up a list of supplies we need to prioritise. Enough for thirty days for thirty people. The other essential supplies are going to make quite a big pile, so let's get it all sorted and loaded and then we'll see if we have space for anything else."

He turned to me. "Tom, while we're doing that, I want you to give some thought to where we should go. You've got the local knowledge and you've spent a lot of time out of the compound on scavenging missions."

I nodded. "OK no problems. What type of location should I be thinking of?"

He thought for a second. "Ideally somewhere remote enough to have escaped the rats. Trees to provide shelter and fuel and nearby fresh water. Anything else we can hopefully bring with us."

"OK, I'm on it." I went back to the Land Rover, pulled out a road atlas and took myself off to a table in the kitchen area. I already had a rough idea of the best area to head for. In theory, the countryside on the south side of the M42 motorway that encircled Birmingham should provide plenty of suitable places; it was just a matter of identifying the best one.

When I glanced up from the map five minutes later, I could see that Paul and Pete had formed a chain gang and my trailer was rapidly filling with a variety of boxes, containers and sacks. I knew I could trust them not to miss anything, even though this was being organised in a huge rush.

I quickly pinpointed a suitable place. It was a small wood surrounded by open countryside. It was less than ten miles away, so even at walking pace it shouldn't take more than three or four hours to get there.

I had vague memories of the wood from driving past it many times over the years.

The map showed a stream flowing through a nearby field and from what I could recall, it was about as good a location as we were likely to get without a more exhaustive and time-consuming search. Time was the one thing we didn't have.

On my return, I noted Harry and Chris busy creating another pile, which consisted of cooking, camping and survival equipment. Another soldier was checking through a smaller but much more dangerous looking pile of guns and ammunition.

Harry looked up as I approached and gestured towards the car. More stuff was being packed on to its roof rack and into the boot. "We're almost there with the supplies." He nodded at the two piles, "We should be able to balance this lot on top. If everyone carries a full Bergen containing their personal stuff and whatever else we need to add before we leave, we should be ready to go."

When I showed them our intended destination Paul nodded, "What are we worrying about? It's only about half an hour away at a steady drive…if we forget anything serious, one of you can always pop back and get it."

Jerry, hurrying past him at the time, overheard him and snapped, "Don't be an idiot, man, three more of us are showing symptoms. I don't want any of you back here until I give the 'all clear'. I'm going to have to give everyone a full check-up before I allow them to leave anyway. We can't risk anyone carrying the disease with them."

Without waiting for a reply, he hurried off, his face careworn and weary. People he considered to be friends were dying and there was nothing he could do about it.

Paul and I looked at each other soberly, and then set to work again loading up the supplies.

CHAPTER TWELVE

True to his word, Jerry carried out a thorough examination on everyone who was planning to leave. Six more people were found to be showing early signs: elevated temperatures, heart rates and blood pressure. They were immediately placed in isolation.

Only time would tell if they had the disease. So far, according to Jerry's records, this particular strain was taking a maximum of one or two days to develop. If after that time the patient didn't develop it, Jerry would agree to them joining the rest of us. In the meantime, those of us who were fortunate enough to have left already would need to keep our masks on for the next few days. Providing the place we fled to was free of the source of the plague (the rats/fleas), we could reasonably assume that we were free of infection, and it would be safe for us to remove the masks.

We all agreed that if anyone developed any symptoms after leaving, they would be isolated as soon as possible and delivered back to the compound. They would have to sit in the back of the empty trailer during the drive to lessen the risk of infecting others.

Paul and the two soldiers confirmed that they would be staying on to guard the compound and help look after the sick, to the best of their abilities.

Although it was left unsaid, we were only too aware that part of this would involve burying the dead.

Harry and Chris were coming with us. Although our knowledge about how to survive in the wild had improved considerably since Chris had begun his training sessions, we knew his expertise would vastly improve our chances.

We were still just "townies" after all. Harry would be assuming responsibility for "security matters".

A few families were now faced with an agonising choice. If one or more of their family members was sick, should they all stay?

Or should one person remain behind to help care for them while the others left for the relative safety of an unknown destination? In the end, if the sick person was an adult, as heart-breaking as it might be, their families reluctantly agreed to leave without them. If, however, the sick person was a child, then one of their adults was chosen to remain. There had been many tough decisions to make since the event, but no parent was prepared to leave their sick child alone.

Somewhat understandably therefore, amidst the frenetic preparations for departure, emotions were running high.

While I was helping to secure the supplies and equipment on the car and the trailer, Paul came over to me.

"I've just been talking to Hereford. They've got an outbreak there as well. They don't know if it came from the rats or the new arrivals, but the first people to come down with it were the ones from the convoy.

This is bad. They're on total lockdown now. No one gets to go in or out, basically."

I stared at him in dismay. "The good news," he continued, "is they've got enough masks and special suits for most of the people above and below ground. They're working on a system of diagnosis and separation for everyone. Hopefully that'll limit the spread.

The bad news is, we really are on our own now; we can't expect any help from the base for the foreseeable future."

"Oh, well." I shrugged. "So we'll be pretty much back to where we were before you showed up and saved us all eh?"

Detecting my sarcasm, he smiled and just said, "Fair point."

Before long we were ready to leave. We knew we couldn't put it off any longer.

The people who were staying waved and smiled, their faces wet with tears. They knew they had a dreadful ordeal ahead of them and that they would probably have to watch their friends and family members die. Those who were departing, walking beside the heavily laden Land Rover as it crawled along, and waving frantically back, must all have been wondering if they would ever return.

And if they did come back, would there be anyone left to welcome them?

Worst of all were the reactions of the smallest children. Larry, Jerry and Fiona's five-year-old, had to be dragged out of his mother's arms and although he finally submitted to holding Becky's hand as she tried to comfort him, he sobbed uncontrollably, straining to look back over his shoulder all the way down the road until the houses were out of sight. Mercifully, his brother Jack was too young to understand what was happening, and was enjoying being carried on Kim's hip as she walked beside Harry.

The dogs ran back and forth barking excitedly, full of joy at the prospect of being allowed to run free again, having been restricted for so long by the stray dogs and the rat epidemic.

We were all in agreement on the route and, as the roads were familiar to us all, we didn't need our maps to guide us there.

Weighed down by the heavy loads on our backs, twenty-five of us: seventeen adults and eight children left our homes behind and walked with heavy hearts into an uncertain future.

CHAPTER THIRTEEN

We made good time and once I'd estimated that we were less than an hour away from our destination, we halted for a rest.

The adults gratefully lowered their rucksacks to the ground and stretched their aching shoulders and muscles. We were all far fitter than we'd been before the event, but some of us, particularly Pete and Mary, who rarely left the road and were also getting on in years, were visibly flagging.

The dogs happily threw themselves down and fell asleep, as if sitting around was a waste of their time and the only way to deal with the boredom was to nap.

While Chris deftly lit a fire and heated up a few kettles of water, the rest of us watched as the kids, who ten minutes previously had been complaining loudly of feeling tired, launched themselves into a game of tig.

In no time at all we all had a brew in our hands and were munching gratefully on the snacks that were being handed round.

The children only agreed to sit by the fire once the chocolate bars were brought out as an inducement. Chocolate was a rare treat. As we removed our masks to eat and drink, we all tried to keep our distance from each other.

At Harry's request, I took out the map so that he could study our destination again.

"If you don't mind, I'll head off on my own for a bit and approach the wood from the other direction. Just to be on the safe side."

No one could argue with his logic.

He finished his tea and carried out a quick communications check to make sure his radio was working, so that we could stay in touch. He then pulled a smaller day sack out of his over-packed Bergen, and putting it on, asked me to stash his Bergen somewhere on the trailer.

Finally, he grabbed his weapon and prepared to leave.

After walking just five paces down the road, to everyone's bemusement, he made a sudden U-turn and walked decisively up to Kim, who was staring at him in astonishment. Before she could speak, he'd removed his mask and hers, grabbed her, and to everyone's delight and her great embarrassment, kissed her passionately.

Releasing her after several seconds, he turned to us, and with a cheeky grin on his face, walked away again saying, "Keep an eye on her, please; she means a lot to me."

Chuckling at Kim's confusion, as she tried not to smile, and tidied herself up, we prepared for the final leg of the journey.

The place looked exactly as I remembered, as we made our way down a narrow country lane about forty minutes later.

A metal farm gate led into a field, which sloped gently up to the woods. Even with its heavy load, I figured the Land Rover should have no problem negotiating the gradient.

Looking at the gate, I realised that it was locked with a heavy-duty chain and padlock.

"Pete, tell me you brought some bolt cutters with us?"

"Tom!" he said, his eyebrows raised in mock outrage, "What do you take me for? Back left corner of the trailer; it should be just under the bag of tarpaulins."

I grinned as Bob, who was standing by the trailer, quickly retrieved them and walked to the gate.

"May I?" he asked.

"Of course, pal. That's if your injuries will let you," I replied, with a straight face.

Bob was an excellent storyteller and a natural entertainer. Although he'd made a full recovery, after being shot during a savage attack by an unfriendly gang on one of our scavenging trips, he was always more than happy to show his scars to a willing listener. His favourite story was how he, and he alone, had saved the community one day, and that only somebody as heroic and immune to pain as he was, could possibly have stood up to the ensuing surgery that was needed to save his life, *without any anaesthetic.*

The story seemed to change and become more dramatic (and to us, more amusing) with every telling.

Our version of his story, which we delighted in relaying to whoever had been listening to him, included a detailed account of how he had shouted and sworn at everyone, while being rolled unceremoniously home in a wheelbarrow and that, in Jerry's opinion, the layers of fat on him had saved him from more serious injury. By this time, Bob would be looking decidedly hangdog and the person listening to the story would be in fits of laughter…

The bolt cutters sliced easily through the chain.

Looking up at the woods perched on top of the small rise, I thought about Harry's caution in wanting to approach from a different direction.

I signalled to Pete, who was taking a turn at driving, to turn off the engine.

I addressed everyone, "What shall we do? I know there's probably no one around but should we reconnoitre it first?"

It didn't take long to agree that the best course of action would be to check it out first.

Six of us (three men and three women) shrugged off our rucksacks and after a quick weapons check, set off up the slope to the woods, holding our weapons across our chests with the muzzles facing downwards, as we'd been trained to do.

I studied the thicker vegetation that naturally grew around the edge of a wood, where there was always more sunlight. Everything looked normal.

I sniffed. A faint but familiar smell came through my mask.
Wood smoke!

Just as I was about to mention it to the others, a voice called out from the thick bushes facing us.

"Stop right there! Don't move! We have eight guns pointing at you."

The training we'd all received from Captain Berry kicked in, and as one, we brought our weapons to our shoulders and lowered our profile by dropping to one knee, searching for the threat through the sights of our rifles.

"We're friendly! Do not fire on us!" I yelled, trying to remain calm. "We mean you no harm, we're just escaping with our families from the Black Death." We were in a very exposed position and if they opened fire we'd be in serious trouble.

The unknown and unseen man responded.

"The Black Death! Do you think I'm stupid? Now, lower your weapons, lay them on the ground and back away from them, or we'll open fire."

"That's not going to happen," I responded immediately, my heart beating fast. We'd been told never to lower our weapons; by doing so, it put you at an immediate disadvantage. If you're following their instructions, you're in their power. As soon as you lower your weapon, they've won.

During training Paul had talked us through situations like this. If they were going to open fire, then invariably they would have done so by now, without warning. Although it might not seem that way now, the fact that we hadn't complied and lowered our weapons, meant that we'd taken the advantage.

The saying "the silence was deafening" seemed very apt at that moment.

The disembodied voice came back with, I felt, a hint of desperation in it. "Do it now! Or else!"

Suddenly, there was a second voice. "I say old chap. Sorry to interrupt you, but unless I'm very much mistaken, there's only one of you, and my gun which, incidentally, is aimed right at your head at the moment, is a lot bigger than that pop gun you're carrying. Now, please be so kind as to place your gun on the ground and step into the open."

At the sound of the familiar voice, relief rushed through my whole body. I could feel the others beginning to relax alongside me.

A few muttered curses and rustling of bushes followed and then Harry's voice could be heard again through the undergrowth.

"It's OK, everyone, he's disarmed."

We maintained our positions, crouching on one knee with weapons raised, as the bushes swayed and a terrified looking man pushed his way through them.

His arms were raised above his head and Harry was standing directly behind him, his weapon pointed at his back. He had the man's shotgun slung over his shoulder.

"Please!" he gasped, his face pale and sweaty, "just take whatever you want, but don't hurt my…" He stopped, realising he had said too much.

We had momentarily relaxed, but the realisation that there were others out there made us all raise our weapons again.

He dropped to his knees.

"Please don't shoot, I beg you. It's only my family back there. My wife and two children."

The poor man was absolutely petrified.

Given how we looked, it was understandable. Most of us were wearing the military-issued clothing we'd been given over the past months, and were kitted out in tactical vests stuffed with extra magazines for the vicious looking assault rifles we carried. And of course, all our faces were completely covered with either gas masks or disposable paper ones.

All in all, we must have looked very intimidating.

Harry shouted at him, undeterred by his demeanour.

"Where are they? Do they have any weapons?"

Given our past experiences, we couldn't afford to take anything at face value.

You had to assume that everything and everyone was a threat until proved otherwise.

The man pointed weakly back at the woods.

"They're hiding. They know only to come out when I call them and tell them it's safe again."

I spoke up. Trying to keep my tone calm and neutral to defuse the tense situation.

"Look, mate. If you're genuine, then trust me, you have absolutely nothing to fear from us. But our families are down there."

I nodded down the hill towards the Land Rover and trailer.

"I need to make sure it's safe for them above all else. Please can you get your family to show themselves."

"How do I know I can trust you?" he asked warily.

"You don't," I said, with a shrug. "But what other choice do you have?"

I watched him struggle to make sense of the situation, but he was too overwrought to see anything but the danger he thought he was in.

"No way," he said stubbornly, "just take what you want and leave. You'll never find them, and I'll die before I tell you where they are."

The man was doing what any of us would do. He was protecting his family at all costs.

You had to admire him; he was terrified and he had seven guns pointing at him but he was still trying to keep his family safe.

I had an idea.

"Look pal, I don't know how else to convince you that we're genuine and we're not a threat to you, but have you looked at who's pointing a gun at your back?"

With a confused and distrustful look on his face, still with his hands held high above his head, he twisted on his knees and risked a look at Harry, who was still standing behind him. Harry lifted his gas mask from his face and grinned at him before replacing it.

The shock of recognition on his face was comical.

"What the …" He stammered and stuttered some more, as his mouth tried to catch up with his racing brain.

Harry slung his weapon over his shoulder and stepped forward, holding his hand out. The man fell back for a moment in confusion, then shook hands.

Still shaking hands, because the man seemed incapable of letting go, Harry helped him up.

"Sir, I assure you our intentions are peaceful. And we can do a lot to help you. Now, if we can just get your family from their hiding place, we can all have a mug of tea and get to know each other. I'm sure you have some interesting stories to tell."

The shock of recognising a member of the royal family, combined with Harry's calm manner and soothing words, seemed to have completely disarmed the man.

"Are we saved? Is it all over?" he stammered.

Harry shook his head, "No, unfortunately it's not over, sir, and as for being saved, as I think I mentioned before, we're looking for shelter in your wood to escape the plague that's sweeping through our community. It's why we're wearing the masks. So, I suppose you'll be offering us sanctuary. But your family must be beside themselves with worry. Shall we go and get them?"

Still too shocked to say anything, the man nodded, and led us into the woods.

We followed him, staying in a tactical formation with our weapons ready. He seemed genuine enough, but we couldn't take the chance of it being a trap.

He still appeared too stunned to take it all in. He kept looking at all of us, particularly Harry of course, as we followed him between the trees. At last we entered a clearing which, by my estimation, must have been close to the centre of the woods, and he came to a halt next to a pile of dead leaves.

He pointed at the leaves.

"I built a bolt hole; there's a trapdoor under the leaves."

"Do you need a hand?" I asked.

He nodded and I stepped forward.

"Toni," he called out, "it's OK, I'm opening the hatch now. There are some people with me but there's no need to be scared."

There was a muffled but nervous sounding reply from the forest floor.

The hatch wasn't heavy. Sweeping the leaves aside, I grabbed one side of it as the man grabbed the other and we lifted it up and clear of the hole underneath.

Three faces, blinking from the sudden increase in light, looked up at us. He wasn't lying; the hidey-hole contained a woman and two children.

The woman quickly passed the children up to her husband and after giving them both a quick hug, he reached down and helped his wife up and out of the hole.

The four of them stood there, staring at us.

I broke the ice.

"Hi, I'm Tom, and these are my friends," I said, indicating the others by my side. "I'm sorry if we gave you a scare but we didn't know anyone was in these woods."

It occurred to me that the rest of our group were still waiting for us and had no idea what was happening. They'd only witnessed our previous exchange from a distance and then the last they'd seen was us trooping off into the woods.

"Pam and William, could you please go and get the others to come up. They must be going out of their minds. Tell them to get the car as close as possible; we can sort things out later."

As the two ran off to speak to the others, the four strangers continued to gape at us in silence. They seemed to be finding it difficult to believe we were real, although in fairness to them, they probably hadn't had any contact with anyone for quite some time. The sudden appearance of dozens of intimidating people carrying weapons and wearing masks would be quite hard to process quickly.

That said, they really needed to snap out of it. "Right, then," I said briskly, "the rest of us will be arriving soon. Do you have a camp or base where it will be more comfortable to meet everyone and maybe get a brew going?"

The man blinked a few times and managed to pull himself together.

"Yes, yes of course. Let me show you to our camp."

We followed them a short distance until we came to another clearing.

I was surprised to see an articulated lorry along one side of the clearing. There were also a number of structures fashioned out of branches and logs arranged around a central fire pit. A large tent had been pitched under a crude, but effective looking shelter, providing additional protection from the elements.

Still looking a little dazed, the man pointed out some chairs arranged around the fire. A large tarpaulin had been suspended above them to provide shelter from the weather.

"Please. Take a seat. I'm sorry we don't have enough chairs."

"Not a problem. Sorry, in all the excitement we didn't get to introduce ourselves properly. I'm Tom, as you know, and you obviously know Harry here. I won't introduce everyone else yet, because it will all get confusing. There'll be plenty of time for that later. What are your names?"

"I'm Steve," he said awkwardly, "Steve Bradley, and this is my wife Toni and my son Logan and daughter Sophie."

A loud whistle from somewhere in the woods interrupted us.

Harry laughed. "They can't find us; I'll go and get them." He turned and walked off in search of the others, disappearing quickly through the trees.

Steve turned to his family, "Listen! You're not going to believe who that is. That's Prince Harry!"

They looked back at him in astonishment. "No!" said Toni.

"Yes, it is!" I said, laughing. "We'll tell you our story later. You may not find some of it believable, but …" I pointed in the direction that Harry had gone, "we do have the evidence to back it all up. I'm sorry if we seem a bit distracted.

We had to leave our home and a lot of our friends and family behind this morning. Most of them are very sick and we're not sure if they'll survive or not."

I reached into a pocket, where I had some spare masks, and handed them to Steve.

"It would be best if you put these on. One of us may be infected but not be showing symptoms."

Steve suddenly looked angry, and was about to say something when I stopped him.

"Look I know what you're about to say. In your situation, I'd probably feel the same, but we've all been examined by a doctor, and I can assure you we're only keeping the masks on until we know we're all clear. You'll be completely safe, believe me. The masks are just a precaution."

By now the rest of our group was arriving, and as the family hurriedly put on their masks and stepped forward, our circle opened up to include them.

"Everyone, this is Steve and Toni and their kids, Logan and Sophie."

The others nodded and smiled and I turned back to Steve.

"Look, it may seem a bit late to ask, but I hope you won't mind if we join you and set up camp in this wood. I'm sure with the supplies and resources we have to offer it would be of huge benefit to you."

Steve looked at his wife, who said nothing, then looked back at all of us. "Well, I suppose realistically I don't have much choice in the matter, but as far as we're concerned, you're all welcome. We haven't seen another soul for months and we sure could do with some help. I don't want to go through another winter like the one we've just had."

Everyone looked relieved. This would be our new home for the foreseeable future.

CHAPTER FOURTEEN

Steve showed us the track he'd used to get the lorry into the woods. After we'd cleared it of the felled trees he'd used to block it, we drove the Land Rover and trailer into the clearing.

Although we were impatient to exchange stories, we agreed to unload and set up first. First and foremost, we needed shelter.

Chris and Harry took over. The plan initially was to set up hammocks under tarpaulin shelters. This was by far the easiest and quickest way to make sure everyone had somewhere warm and comfortable to sleep.

Chris had taught us well, and in no time at all the tarpaulins were up and the hammocks were hung between suitable trees. The children greeted the prospect of sleeping under the stars with great excitement, but the mood among the adults was rather more subdued. We couldn't help wondering what our people were going through back at the compound.

The masks made any sort of physical work uncomfortable and slowed our pace considerably, but eventually most of the stuff we'd brought with us had been unloaded, and under Pete's supervision, had been set up or stacked in orderly piles.

While we carried out Chris's instructions, Harry, whose primary concern was now security, checked out the woods and the surrounding area. He returned an hour later with a list of jobs he needed help with. He'd decided to build look-out posts at strategic places and create some defensible positions we could use if we were attacked. This would all take some doing, but the basics could be completed relatively quickly and then improved upon over time.

Harry commandeered a few willing helpers and, gathering some equipment, they trudged off into the woods to make a start.

Steve and his family were going out of their way to be helpful, and although we'd found out the hard way that it was not a good idea to trust strangers, before long we decided they were genuine enough and we felt that they would fit in well.

We were about to call it a day, as we felt we'd accomplished enough to make us all comfortable and everyone was now emotionally and physically exhausted, when Pete turned up looking pale and serious.

"William, can I have a word?" he said quietly, and we watched uneasily as he placed his hand on his shoulder and took him to one side. We all knew that William had been forced to leave the compound with his two oldest children while his youngest, Adam, had remained behind with his wife.

Pete spoke too softly for us to hear but the message was clear. William let out a heart wrenching wail and fell to his knees, sobbing. His two older children, James and Heather, hung back miserably, tears streaming down their faces.

Unable to bear the sight I turned to Becky, who was weeping quietly, and we held each other for comfort.

We were all devastated by the news of Adam's death, and those who had left people behind experienced renewed feelings of terror about what the future might hold for them.

To make matters worse, Pete quietly explained that Jerry was expecting more deaths before too long. Despite all his efforts, there was little he could do for them medically. All he and his helpers could do was try to make the patients as comfortable as possible.

Only Allan seemed to be holding his own. Perhaps he had acquired some natural immunity somehow. But the thought of him fighting was some consolation to us.

Leaving William, James and Heather to deal with their pain as best they could, the rest of us, exhausted and drained, gathered quietly around the campfire, which was now blazing cheerfully.

Its light and warmth offered us some small comfort in the growing gloom.

Toni had thoughtfully made a large pot of stew from her own supplies to feed us all, and we queued up gratefully, clutching our mess tins. Then we returned to the fireside to eat, most of us lost in our own thoughts. William and his children joined us briefly for some food, managed a little, and then headed off sadly to their sleeping area.

It didn't take long to get the exhausted children off to sleep.

Although we were all incredibly weary, most of us were reluctant to turn in. The knowledge that we were likely to receive more bad news in the morning weighed heavily on our minds. I suppose by putting off going to bed, we were hoping to delay the inevitable.

And we also wanted to tell Steve and Toni our story and listen to theirs.

I began, with several other people chipping in at opportune moments, and together we gave Steve and Toni an abridged version of everything that had happened to us so far, promising to fill them in on the details over the next few days.

Having told our story to various people over time, it was now finely honed, and it wasn't long before they were fully appraised of what had happened to us and what, to the best of our knowledge, had been happening in the wider world.

They were horrified to learn of the expected death toll nationally, but somewhat cheered by the news that the majority of the survivors were working jointly with what was left of the government to try to rebuild.

For the most part they listened without comment, asking a few pertinent questions here and there, but otherwise just absorbing all the information we were giving them.

When we'd finished, Steve told us what had happened to them.

Steve had been an owner/operator lorry driver. In other words, he'd owned his own lorry and hauled goods on a contract basis for several companies.

The previous year, about a week before the event, he'd been overjoyed to receive out of the blue, a contract to start hauling goods for a company at what appeared to be fantastic rates. The company was also offering large bonuses for early acceptance and for any driver completing more runs than specified in the contract.

It all seemed too good to be true, but after quickly investigating the company on the internet, he'd been satisfied that they were legitimate and had quickly accepted the contract.

From day one, his suspicions were aroused. He was using his tractor unit to pick up trailers from supermarket food distribution warehouses and delivering them to locations received via his phone, which he was required to check regularly for instructions.

He'd hauled from these places in the past when supermarkets needed extra capacity at busy times such as Christmas. But this level of activity was unprecedented.

Everyone seemed to be in a rush and the logistics involved in keeping all the extra rigs and trailers moving in a coordinated fashion was impressive. Furthermore, there always seemed to be a few military people around.

Whenever he asked what was going on, he was always told the same thing: there had been a massive computer failure at other similar warehouses across the country. The remaining ones were having to cover all those locations and the government had sent in their logistics experts to help, hence the uniforms.

At one point, he received an email from the company advising that, due to exceptional circumstances, if he found himself exceeding his tachograph hours to complete the job, he should not be concerned. The government had classified the work as being "in the national interest" and therefore any tachograph transgressions would be disregarded.

This really shocked him, as the email was more or less stating that it was OK to break the law.

He explained that in the UK, commercial vehicles were fitted with devices called tachographs which continually monitored and recorded the lorry's activity. This ensured that drivers didn't break the strict laws on hours worked and speed exceeded etc.

The story was plausible enough I suppose, if you didn't have an enquiring mind. And the longer hours would mean a lot more money.

After two days of hauling from food distribution points, he received instructions to start hauling containers from docks.

The UK had always imported vast quantities of food. We were, after all, a small island with a large population, and for decades it had not been possible for us to produce enough to feed ourselves. Without the container ships constantly delivering a huge variety of foodstuffs, we would have starved.

Steve was aware of this, and happily continued with the contract, all the time planning what he would spend the extra money on.

Everything was going well until he blew a tyre on an A road on the way to drop a container. It was to be his first drop at this location and he was mystified by it. The satellite navigation system had directed him to a field in the middle of open countryside. Then the instructions he had received on his phone had advised him to trust the directions.

He had also been instructed that, in the event of a breakdown he should contact the office and they would dispatch their own recovery company. After inspecting his shredded tyre and realising that he needed help, he called the number he'd been given and reported his location.

He was politely told to wait. Someone would be with him as soon as possible.

From experience, he was prepared for a long wait. He used a portable stove to boil up some water for a cup of coffee, and relaxed in his cab. About twenty minutes later he was surprised to see a recovery truck approaching and he was even more taken aback when two soldiers carrying sidearms stepped out of the cab and approached him.

He was astounded that he was receiving roadside assistance from the military, so of course he was full of questions. To begin with, the soldiers seemed unwilling to talk and set about changing the wheel, but the more he talked to them, the more they began to open up.

They had been working as vehicle mechanics with the Royal Electrical and Mechanical Engineers when they'd suddenly been mobilised, given requisitioned recovery trucks, and sent to locations to await breakdowns. He was their first, so they had been wondering if it was some sort of exercise and had been naturally suspicious of "the man in the broken-down truck".

Once they had established that he was genuine, and was just a bloke in need of assistance, they relaxed and began to talk.

They were just as confused as him. They were in touch with friends in other regiments; some had been mobilised like them, and some were carrying on as if nothing had happened.

They reported dozens of lorries, loaded mainly with foodstuffs, delivering to a huge newly constructed area where they were being asked to wait until they were needed. The loads were then split up and sent on their way.

Lots of rumours were flying about but the most common one, and the one that appealed to them most, was that something catastrophic was going to happen in the next few days and all this effort was to get food to where it was going to be needed most. Knowing that most rumours in the military, although exaggerated, are usually based on fact, they realised that this one was probably true.

Before long, Steve's truck was roadworthy again, and with more questions than answers, he continued on to his destination.

As soon as he arrived he knew that something big was happening.

The so-called "field" he had been directed to was an immense, recently built hardstanding, where containers of foodstuffs were rapidly being unloaded, split up and loaded back on to other vehicles that were standing by.

It was exactly as the soldiers had described it.

As he helped himself to a cup of coffee from a mobile canteen, he tried talking to the other drivers to find out if they knew what was going on. The majority were only interested in the money they were earning, and were reluctant to ask questions, in case it jeopardised the gravy train they had found themselves on.

A few admitted they had queried what was going on, but they had been told to shut up and get on with their jobs.

Worried and even more confused, he finished his last run and made his way home.

That evening, once the children were in bed, he talked everything through with Toni.

At first, she was dismissive but she quickly realised how serious he was. She suggested that he should try to find out more the following day.

The next day he was asked to haul a container from the docks to the same location as the day before. After he had dropped his trailer and was waiting for his next load, he happened to glance through the window of one of the portacabins and noticed a man sitting alone at a desk. He was in uniform and looked reasonably senior.

He decided to go for broke and try to find out what was really going on.

He knocked firmly on the door, entered the portacabin and politely and calmly introduced himself to the officer. He described everything he'd heard and witnessed over the last few days and asked, for the sake of himself and his family, if he would kindly explain it all.

The officer looked at him for a full minute in silence. Then he stood up and locked the door to his office and motioned for Steve to sit down.

Then he told him what he knew.

The officer (Steve never found out his name) admitted that he had been wrestling with his own conscience for some time over this. Even he hadn't been given all the facts, but he had managed to piece most of it together from the snippets of information he had garnered himself. He had only had it confirmed that very morning, when he had confronted his own commanding officer.

He insisted that it was not that the military and the government were keeping secrets; there just hadn't been time to inform everyone. The main priority had been to secure as much of the nation's food supplies as possible so that it could be distributed as part of the planned relief effort.

The order had just come through for them to return to base, along with the food-filled lorries that had been allocated to them. There were no more supplies to be distributed. Every major food distribution hub had been emptied and every delivery of food into the country that could possibly be identified, either by air or sea, had been diverted.

He had received no instructions on how to deal with the civilian contractors who had been working for them, or even what to say to them. This oversight, he assured Steve, had been due to the panic and chaos of the past few days. There had literally been no time to think about it.

Steve's visit had forced the officer to come to a decision. He told him that he intended to try to warn as many people as possible. Steve reminded him that he had a responsibility towards everyone who had been working so hard towards the government's cause. They had a right to know.

He explained that at some point on Friday 10 October (the very next day in fact) as the Earth spun on its axis around the sun, the entire planet was going to be hit by a massive Coronal Mass Ejection, which would spew forth from the sun.

The likely severity of the effects was still being widely debated, but the government had chosen to err on the side of caution and assume the worst: that there would be worldwide power disruptions when the grid went down.

This could potentially have an impact on the distribution of food, so a nationwide food distribution system had hastily been set up, requisitioning food in the hope that they would have sufficient to feed everyone until the power (if it went off at all) could be restored.

According to his commanding officer, a lot of senior people were very sceptical about the severity of the effects postulated in some of the reports that had been commissioned. They were therefore less than enthusiastic about ensuring that the orders were being followed. They believed that it would all be a complete waste of time, effort and resources, and that once the predicted event failed to materialise, heads were likely to roll. This would give them an opportunity to further their own careers.

Steve asked the officer what he thought about it all, having rapidly come to the conclusion that this was a man with intelligence and integrity; someone whose opinion could be relied upon. The officer thought for a moment and then told him his gut instinct was telling him that the government would not be going to this much effort unless there was no other option on the table. The amount of money expended over the past few days must now have run into hundreds of millions of pounds.

He knew the way the military and the government worked, and he was very worried.

When Steve asked him what to do, he shrugged and suggested he do what he thought best. In his opinion, as of tomorrow, *when* the predicted event happened, before long every supermarket and food outlet would be stripped of its contents. There would be mass panic once the public realised that food supplies were running out and were not likely to be replaced.

And despite the massive quantity of foodstuffs that had been stockpiled as part of the aid plan, as a soldier he had worked on disaster relief missions across the globe, and he knew how easily things could fall apart. Although the stockpiles were huge, once they were divided among millions of hungry civilians, they were not likely to last long at all.

At this point, his head spinning, Steve thanked the officer, left the office and climbed into his cab where he could sit in peace and decide what to do next.

He never saw the officer again.

His mind only began to clear once he'd been given his next delivery. He was told to drop the trailer he was about to hook up at another depot. Once that was done, it would be his last run of the day, and he was to await instructions for the following day.

Looking around the site, he realised that there was little left to shift. Very few lorries had arrived with new loads, and what the officer had told him began to ring true.

All the available food had been requisitioned. There was nothing left.

If this event did happen. When all the packets, tins and sacks of food had gone. Well that would be it. If you couldn't grow it or catch it, you'd starve to death and your family would starve along with you.

Then the answer came to him and suddenly everything seemed clear.

He had a family to look after and he had a lorryload of food on his trailer. Literally thousands of tonnes of food had been moved over the past few days; no one could possibly keep track of it all. If his one insignificant little load didn't make it to its destination, who would actually know?

The risk, he decided, was worth it. His primary concern had to be his family. To be given privileged information and not act upon it would be a crime. If the predicted event didn't happen, he would just be a day late with his load and would make up a vaguely plausible explanation if he was missed at all.

Decision made, he called Toni as he drove.

He knew they couldn't just park a lorry full of food outside his house. It wouldn't take people long to find out what was in it and that would put them at unnecessary risk. They needed to hide the lorry somewhere where only they would have access to it.

It was Toni who suggested that they hide the lorry in the countryside somewhere. They often went camping as a family; it was a good way to holiday on a budget. A few years before, they had decided that, rather than blowing all their hard-earned holiday savings on two weeks in the sun, it would be better for the family to take more frequent, shorter breaks, and the best way to do that was by going camping. They'd invested in good quality camping equipment to make the experience as comfortable as possible and had enjoyed great family breaks exploring England, Wales and Scotland.

They agreed between them that Toni would get the children out of school early and start putting together all the equipment they would need, while Steve, on the drive home, would try to think of the best place for them to go.

The woods sprang immediately to mind. The year before, on one of their regular Sunday cycling trips, they had stopped there and had a picnic in the woods. It had been a hot summer's day and he remembered the gate they had chained their bikes to and the gentle slope they had climbed to reach the woods. The lorry should have no trouble reaching them.

Some of their neighbours grumbled when he parked his lorry outside the house, but in no time at all they had loaded up everything they could think of and he and his family were on their way.

Toni had explained as much as she could to the kids about what they thought might happen and what they were planning to do. They had been excited by the prospect of an adventure and eager to help with the preparations.

He had taken the opportunity to inspect the load he was carrying once he had pulled up outside the house. He was relieved to see that it contained pallets stacked high with tins of meat, vegetables and fruit. There wasn't much variety, and given the amount, they would probably be bored with it before long, but they certainly wouldn't go hungry for a long time.

In view of the dry weather, and based on years of experience driving lorries in all conditions, Steve had no trouble driving the lorry up the slope and into the woods along the overgrown track. Once they arrived they spent the rest of the day, and most of the following, setting up camp and trying to conceal any traces of the lorry having climbed the slope and entered the woods.

The event, when it happened, passed by unnoticed until Logan tried to turn on his iPod in the afternoon and couldn't get it to work. A quick check of everything else, including the lorry, confirmed it. Steve set out on his bicycle to see what was happening and encountered disorder and confusion.

The roads were full of broken-down vehicles and stranded motorists.

They knew they were incredibly lucky to have been given the chance to prepare themselves. Who knew what the next weeks or months might bring?

In the end, although they hadn't made a conscious decision to hide, they did try to live in the woods as quietly and unobtrusively as possible. Instinctively, they knew it would be best not to advertise their presence. They also knew that it wouldn't take long for people to start running out of food, and were only too aware of the value of the lorry's contents.

Hopefully, the planned relief effort would help, but given what the officer had said about how long the stockpiled food was likely to last, they realised that people might become desperate. And desperate people do desperate things.

They talked long into the night, wrestling with their consciences and wondering if they should be offering people help.

In the end, they decided that if anyone discovered them they would try to give the impression that they were barely surviving. It would be impossible to hide the truck so they would say it had been abandoned before they'd arrived in the woods. They would share what they had on them but would not advertise the existence of their hidden bounty.

For the first week or so, everything was quiet. They settled in well, and Steve used the tools he had brought and his DIY skills to make the camp as comfortable as possible.

Gradually over time, they emptied the lorry and buried the contents in hidden stashes all over the woods.

Throughout this time, they kept a lookout for other people. Occasionally people could be seen, either on their own or as a group, in the lane below the woods.

Four weeks later, everything changed.

Steve was retrieving food from a stash at the other side of the woods, when an unnoticed group cycling along the lane spotted the smoke from the campfire rising through the trees.

They headed straight for the campsite, surprising Toni and the children, who had been busy preparing food. The group consisted of four men. One of them was carrying a shotgun.

From the outset, their behaviour was intimidating. They demanded to know who else was with them and where they were keeping their food, and made lewd comments about Toni and Sophie. Logan tried to push in front of his mother and sister in a brave attempt to protect them, and was punched in the face for his trouble.

Steve, oblivious to what was happening, was returning to camp when he heard the men's voices. Placing the bag of food he'd been carrying on the ground, and resisting the urge to barge straight in, he approached as quietly as possible. He was still carrying the shovel he'd been using to unearth the food.

When he got to the camp, it soon became clear that they were all in serious trouble. Armed only with a shovel, there was no way he could possibly overpower all four of the men, particularly the one with the shotgun.

He thought about going for the armed man first, but there was no guarantee he would be able to grab the weapon before one of the others did. He needed to bide his time and pick his moment.

He knew that his family were aware that he was out there, but the attackers didn't, and that was his only advantage. One wrong move could squander his only chance of success.

He watched helplessly as his son again tried to protect his mother and sister. One of the men laughed mockingly and knocked him flying, letting out a torrent of abuse as he did so.

Finally, his patience was rewarded. The man with the shotgun sent one of his companions to find the other members of their group who, it seemed, were still searching the nearby village of Tanworth in Arden.

There had been little left to steal there, so the four of them had set off in search of other victims and better pickings. After all, the leader called after him, as he walked away laughing, the others might not see their bikes and might cycle straight past this place.

Then they'd miss out on all the fun, he added, a sneering look on his face.

At this point, Steve realised he was going to have to fight them.

"Tell the boss I found her first, I get first go!"

His heart pounding, Steve knew this would be his only chance. He watched as the man walked off, noted the direction he was taking, and using his knowledge of the woods, ran hell for leather to the point where he would appear. The woods were dense and there were few paths through them. He had to head him off.

Holding his breath, he hid behind a tree as the man walked past. He closed his eyes for a split second, said a silent prayer, stepped out and swung the heavy shovel with all his might at the man's head. There was no time for subtlety; his family was in danger.

The man dropped to the ground dead, the back of his head caved in, spraying blood all over Steve.

Steve, the blood pumping in his ears, turned and sprinted back again.

He knew he would have to end this situation soon and the only way he could do this was by overpowering the others as quickly as possible. He would have to throw caution to the wind, go for it, and hope for the best. If just one of them escaped, they'd bring all the rest of the gang back with them and there was no way he would be able to fight them all.

One man, armed only with a shovel and attitude, was about to take on three men, one of whom was armed with a shotgun.

The only thing on Steve's side was the element of surprise. He had to get to the bloke with the gun first.

He ran full pelt into the clearing with his shovel raised. The man with the gun had his back to him.

Screaming with an almost primordial rage, he smashed the man's skull in, spraying more blood over himself.

The other two men, staring open mouthed, and faced with the prospect of a blood-soaked madman who had come from nowhere and virtually decapitated their leader, were rooted to the ground with shock. Their shock rapidly turned to terror, when Steve turned and ran at them, still screaming and swearing like a man possessed.

One of them turned and ran into a tree, knocking himself out, but the other, who was lighter on his feet, headed for the trees, screaming for help.

In the meantime, Toni, who had never held any kind of weapon, let alone fired one before, ran forward and grabbed the gun, which was still lying beside the dead man. Holding it awkwardly, and shaking badly, she pointed it towards the last man as he ran. The single shot almost knocked her off her feet but in spite of her wild aim, some of the pellets hit him in the leg and he stumbled and fell, crying out in pain. His cries abruptly cut off as Steve, who had set off in pursuit, hit him with the shovel.

Scarcely able to believe what he'd managed to do, he dropped the shovel and fell to his knees panting. His family gathered round him, and they all embraced, crying in fear and relief.

Three men, and possibly a fourth, had just died by his hand and all he felt was relief that his family were safe.

The man who had knocked himself out was still unconscious, so they tied him up tightly and gagged him.

Toni remembered in panic that the rest of the gang would be cycling past at any minute. The men they had overpowered must have had bikes too. Where did they leave them?

They thought fast. Surely they wouldn't have hidden them? They might still be in plain sight on the road, advertising where they'd gone to one and all.

Realising which gate they'd probably used to access the field, Steve set out at a full sprint. There was no time to lose. As he ran down the slope, he spotted four bikes leaning casually up against the gate.

As he was lifting the first bike over the gate, he thought he heard a sound and stopped, listening.

His heart missed a beat. He could hear voices in the distance. It had to be the rest of the gang approaching. Panic-stricken, he looked up the lane. They hadn't come around the corner yet, but they couldn't be far away.

He threw the bike he was holding over the gate and quickly followed it with the others.

Diving over the gate, he just managed to fling the bikes and himself out of sight against the hedge before the first gang member sped past on a bike. Burying his face in the ground and trying to make himself as small as possible he barely breathed, as by his estimation, twenty or so bikes sped past, their owners hollering and cussing each other, like a bunch of rowdy mates out on a leisurely Sunday afternoon ride.

He was about to stand up when a few stragglers passed, shouting and swearing at the front runners to slow down and let them catch up.

It took him a few minutes to be sure that there were no more of them, and to get his heart rate to slow down enough for him to stand up and make his way back to his family.

But there was no time to relax. They had a mess to clean up.

The bound and gagged man had died as well. Steve didn't stop to dwell on it, but he suspected that in their panic, they had gagged him too tightly and he had suffocated. Part of him was relieved that he wouldn't have to decide what to do with him. He didn't want to think about it.

All he needed to decide now was where to bury them.

Exhausted though they were, the rest of the day was spent dragging the bodies to a clearing away from the campsite and digging a hole big enough and deep enough to accommodate them.

The rucksacks and pockets of the dead gang members had produced a few useful supplies, and tools such as knives, but by far the most valuable addition to their possessions was the shotgun and twenty cartridges.

Their only means of defence before had been to hide away and avoid drawing attention to themselves. Now that they had a shotgun, Steve felt they would have the upper hand if anyone else approached them.

It was only later that night, when the children were finally asleep, that the reality of it all caught up with him. He had killed four people. He sobbed quietly, while Toni did her best to comfort him.

He knew they had been lucky, not only to survive their recent encounter, but also to have the means to survive in this new world that seemed to be emerging. It was now patently clear that no one was coming to rescue them.

If they were going to live, it was up to them.

As the months passed, the temperatures dropped and winter set in. Now all their efforts as a family were focused on surviving.

Cutting, gathering and splitting enough dry wood to keep the fire going was a continual job for one person.

It was the only way to keep warm, sterilise water and cook the food they had. Without it they would die. The wood needed to be as dry as possible, to keep the smoke to a minimum and avoid attracting unwanted attention.

It was not possible, with only four people, to keep a lookout at all times, but at most times during daylight one of the family would walk the perimeter of the woods, keeping out of sight.

As a way of attracting someone's attention without shouting, Steve used long lengths of wire stripped from the surrounding fences to rig up a crude but effective warning system. At various points around the perimeter, wires suspended between trees stretched back to the camp, terminating at bunches of tin cans tied together. Whichever bunch rattled, indicated what direction a potential threat might be coming from.

The care they had taken to conceal their presence in the woods had paid off. Few people were spotted passing by, and fewer still even glanced at the woods.

It was rarer still for anyone to approach and if they did, Steve fell back on the technique he'd tried with us: intimidation and threats to scare them away.

Once or twice it was obvious that the people approaching them were in dire need and they did agree to help them. They offered them the chance to rest and recover for a while, so that they could continue on their journey.

The first family they felt compelled to help were a couple carrying their two young children in child backpacks. They were utterly exhausted and at the end of their endurance.

To begin with Steve tried to drive them away, pretending that they had nothing themselves. But the tears and desperation they showed as they turned dejectedly away, with their children crying on their backs, was more than Toni could bear. She called out to them to stop and they followed them gratefully into the woods.

Their story was fairly typical.

They had tried to stay at home for as long as possible and had witnessed their neighbourhood degenerating into a place of violence. They had eked out their diminishing food supplies for as long as possible, and using some knowledge, supplemented what they had by harvesting what they could from their own and other gardens, and the local parks.

Most of their neighbours had fled in fear, hoping to find help elsewhere, and the whole area had fallen to the gangs, who robbed, terrorised and killed the few who remained. Aware that this was happening, they had secured their house to the best of their abilities, hoping that the gangs would leave them be, in preference to easier targets elsewhere.

They had known it wouldn't last.

A gang of men had eventually broken in and they had barely managed to scare them away after a desperate fight in the hallway of their house. Grabbing the bags they had ready and carrying the children on their backs, they had fled.

They had family in Devon so they had decided to try to reach them.

They told them about the horrors they had encountered: of ramshackle camps full of starving people, dead bodies littering the pavements, and of hiding in terror from roving gangs, as they struggled to make their way south. The more they heard, the more Steve and Toni realised how ridiculously lucky they had been to have found this place and to have avoided discovery.

When they told them this, the couple were quick to warn them that, according to people they had spoken to, they were living in an area controlled by a gang from Redditch. People they had met had warned them about this gang, urging them to keep out of their way at all costs, as they would show them no mercy if they found them.

With a shock of recognition, I realised that they were almost certainly talking about Gumin and his gang.

I interrupted Steve at this point, as it seemed like a pertinent time to tell him about them, and explained how they had hopefully been wiped out once we had discovered their base.

They nodded, saying that they recalled hearing distant explosions and the rattle of automatic gunfire a few months previously. We agreed that that was probably the day of our attack.

The young family ended up staying with them for several days, as it was clear that they posed no threat and could really do with some help. They did consider asking them to stay, but the couple were determined to try to find their family in Devon, explaining that the place they were aiming for was reasonably remote and hopefully therefore, safer. Their relatives had run the place as a smallholding, growing a lot of their own vegetables and keeping a few chickens and other animals.

It sounded perfect, and the thought of reaching this potential nirvana had kept them going beyond the point of exhaustion.

But it was clear that they had reached the limits of their endurance and would need several days of rest and food before they could continue.

Steve and Toni watched sadly, as they finally set out, carrying their two young children and as much food as they could manage. They hoped fervently that they would make it.

As winter tightened its grip, they rarely saw other people and all their efforts went into trying to survive the biting and constant cold.

When the thaw came, their initial joy and relief at having survived the winter, almost immediately gave way to despair. They knew that they couldn't realistically get through another winter living in the woods. They would need to find a more permanent location for the future.

Since that time, not one person had passed by the woods. We received this news soberly. It didn't say much for the fate of the rest of the population.

They had almost dropped dead with shock at the sight of us approaching, particularly given how intimidating we looked. For the first time, Steve had felt it necessary to order his family into the secret hideaway they had dug. A shelter of last resort.

He admitted that when he'd hugged them before leaving them behind to confront us, he'd been convinced it was for the last time.

Stories exchanged, we turned in for the night.

CHAPTER FIFTEEN

News received in the morning, from home and from the base, did nothing to raise our spirits.

More people had died overnight and the ones who were still alive were deteriorating fast. One or two of our group who had lost loved ones, had to be physically restrained from trying to return home. But there was nothing they could do and they still had the family who were with them to look after. Their grief was raw and tangible. All we could do was try to comfort them.

Until the last of the sickness had passed, no one from home could be allowed to join us without being quarantined first. Despite still being symptom-free, we were sufficiently worried that we had all agreed to wear our masks for at least a few more days. In the meantime, the enforced separation from our friends and family back at the compound, though necessary, was beginning to take its toll.

The only good news was that none of the volunteers who had stayed behind to care for the sick, or guard the compound, had fallen ill. Similar circumstances were being reported from the base, where cases of the plague were on the increase.

Although they had taken steps to seal the underground base, this had failed to keep out the disease, and even over the radio, we could tell from Colonel Moore's voice that the strain was starting to tell.

Despite all their resources and their eminent qualifications, their doctors were losing the battle to find a cure, or even to stop the spread of the disease.

The only way to be safe was to avoid being bitten by an infected flea from a rat, or to avoid close contact with someone who was infected. It was highly contagious and virulent and there was no effective treatment. Only the lucky few who appeared to have some natural resistance, had any chance of survival.

Over at the base, hundreds of soldiers were scouring the place, armed with a variety of weapons, from air rifles to machine guns and grenades, and exterminating every rat they could find.

To make matters worse, communication had been lost with the other royal family members and their staff at Balmoral and they now feared the worst. An overflight from a drone had not revealed any signs of life and plans for a land mission were currently underway.

Harry had been told of this in the previous night's communication, but appeared to be taking the potential loss of his father stoically.

Chris, in a bid to distract us all from our worries, was working us hard on improving the shelters and had introduced various other projects to make life at the camp more pleasant. One of these related to the building of an aerobic composting toilet.

To say that the current system of disposing of waste was basic was an understatement. This involved the use of a rudimentary pit which, when it became too obnoxious, was filled in and replaced by another.

Under Chris's instruction therefore, a raised platform was built with a hole where the air flowing over the deposits below would dry it out. A simple urine catcher drained the liquid waste away elsewhere. If it was kept dry, it would be unlikely to smell, and hopefully, the waste material would rot down over time.

A modesty screen and a roof were added for cosmetic reasons and a lattice work of sticks hid the waste from view.

Harry had thrown himself into improving our security arrangements, and with a few volunteers, was completing the lookout post and defensible positions he had started on the day before.

From what Steve and Toni had told us, few people had been seen since the winter had ended, and therefore we didn't expect much trouble, but the work served to keep everyone busy and distracted. Besides, we'd all learned the hard way not to leave ourselves unprotected and vulnerable. It would be a foolish risk to take.

As a group we were comfortable together and the decision-making process had evolved over time. We now knew who was best qualified to make a judgement on a matter, and often deferred to them on any final decision. But if a discussion on the merits of various options was needed, then we were all agreed that democracy should rule and a simple vote would decide the matter.

The system wasn't perfect, of course, and occasionally you had to bite your tongue if you didn't agree with a chosen option, but as grown-ups we had learned to accept this and move on.

As Steve and his family had lived there first, and were in our eyes the legitimate "owners", we considered ourselves to be his guests. For this reason, we tended to defer to him on most things and we usually sought his approval.

This situation continued for some days until finally he set matters straight.

He'd had little contact with anyone in senior authority and, understandably, was still struggling with how to relate to Harry.

As a result, when Harry approached him one evening by the campfire and attempted to consult him about the two options he was considering for positioning a new lookout post, his reaction left Harry somewhat taken aback.

He stood up in exasperation and shouted, "Look, just stop it everyone, please!"

We all stopped what we were doing and gazed at him in astonishment.

"Look," he said pleadingly, "I'm just a bloody lorry driver. You don't have to ask my permission to do anything. You all have as much right to be here as we do! And yes, I will be telling my grandchildren in years to come about the time I was consulted by Prince Harry about the best place to put a toilet."

He chuckled.

"And I know he hasn't asked me that specific question, but that's the story I'm going to stick to, because it sounds much funnier than a blinking lookout post, and if you don't like it you can…"

He looked round at us and grinned at our worried faces. "Look, just stop asking me for permission, will you? I'm just grateful you're all here, and even more grateful for the coffee and sugar you brought with you. We ran out of those after about a week!" he said, sitting down again. "And now I can have my regulation mug in the morning, you can do what the heck you like!" he added, folding his arms and stretching his legs out.

As we all breathed a sigh of relief and started to smile, Harry winked at us, fixed him with a severe look, and in his best plummy tones said, "Steve, what about the toilet? Can you hurry up and make a choice please? I'm desperate and can't hold it much longer!"

The ensuing laughter was much needed.

CHAPTER SIXTEEN

The following day brought more dreadful news from home. Except for Allan, who was still clinging on, the others had all died overnight.

By now we had all learned not to hope, and most of us received the latest news with numb acceptance. Even the people directly related to the victims were mostly calm, having prepared themselves for the worst. Devastating though the news was, it had come as no surprise, and for most of them at least, the agonising wait was now over; their worst fears had been realised and the grieving process could begin. They gathered together and kept apart from the rest of us for a time, and we left them to mourn in private.

The news from the base was grim and consistent with our own. Most of the people who had contracted the disease had died. About twenty five percent of the deceased were recent arrivals.

Countrywide the death rate was likely to be much higher. We knew we had Jerry to thank for his quick diagnosis. This had enabled us to take the most basic precaution of issuing masks as soon as possible. There was no doubt that this had saved many of us from becoming infected. The same, unfortunately, could not be said for the other communities scattered across the country, who we'd been unable to warn in time.

A conference radio call was set up between the three locations to agree on a set procedure to follow, now that the disease appeared to be burning itself out. All the medical professionals taking part, Jerry included, were vehemently in favour of keeping the quarantine period in place for at least another two weeks.

After all, although the measures taken to quarantine all suspected cases and the obligatory use of surgical masks appeared to have halted the spread of it, it could still be present. Only the passage of time would ensure that it didn't return.

Somewhat reluctantly, the medics had finally given into pressure, and agreed that masks could be dispensed with among the groups who had not had a new arrival, or an occurrence of the disease within the last seven days.

So far, we were the only group that fell into that category, and we compromised over the removal of the masks by designating one person among us to complete hourly checks on everyone and to report any of the danger signs: raised temperatures or sweaty, clammy exposed skin.

Although we all longed to see the people we had left behind, realistically it was likely to be at least two weeks before that happened. The reunion, when it finally took place, would be an emotional one. We tried to curb our impatience by keeping ourselves busy, working furiously on improving our environment, even though we weren't planning to stay for long.

A few days later we received a request to check in on the group that now occupied Gumin's old base at the food distribution warehouse. They had been hit hard by the plague and in their last radio communication, had reported several deaths and about a third of their community infected.

Concerns were growing, as they'd missed the last two radio checks. The first one might possibly be explained away by the pressures of caring for their sick, but after two days of radio silence something needed to be done. In terms of sending out a team to investigate, we were the obvious choice. For one thing, we were the only group now free of infection. For another, we were easily the closest; only a couple of miles away as the crow flies.

We agreed without hesitation and passed on the planning of the mission to Harry.

Half an hour later we were gathered round him and he began his briefing.

While he stood quietly, waiting for us to settle down, it occurred to me that he looked every bit the warrior prince.

I glanced over at Kim and grinned to myself. She seemed to be hypnotised by the sight of him, resplendent in his full battle kit, and exuding an air of authority and confidence.

We were accustomed to seeing him in uniform and the women still talked about how good he had looked in the full-dress uniform he had worn on New Year's Eve. This was, I suspected, partly to tease Kim.

As if she'd read my thoughts, Becky broke the silence by hissing loudly, "Kim, if you haven't decided yet, hurry up. I know the competition isn't as strong as it was, but damn girl, he looks fine in that kit! If Tom wasn't the man he was I'd be tempted myself!"

As the people around us erupted into giggles, she looked over at me. I had been working with Chris and Russ on a water filtration and delivery system. My clothes were spattered with mud and I was looking decidedly dishevelled.

She sighed and rolled her eyes. "In fact, can I change my mind...?"

By now Kim and Harry were both looking decidedly red in the face and people were snorting with laughter.

Having masterfully regained his self-composure, Harry held up his hands for quiet and the briefing began.

"Folks, this mission should be an easy one. The group at the food warehouse has been out of touch for over two days now." He paused and let this sink in, before continuing.

"Best-case scenario: they're all fine and their radio, for some reason, is inoperative. If that is the case, we'll use precautions to avoid infection, and sort out the problem or at least plan to do so in the future. Hopefully, we'll find that they're managing the disease and most of them are still well."

His tone changed and his face darkened.

"Worst-case scenario: the plague has spread out of control and most of them are ill, dead or dying. If that is the case, then experience tells us there won't be much we can do for them. But the question I want to ask you all is: would you be prepared to help relieve the suffering of people we know only distantly, knowing that they are likely to die anyway, and expose yourselves to unnecessary risk?"

Silence greeted this question.

"Obviously," he continued, "only people with full masks will be permitted anywhere near the infected, and if we have any concerns, some or all of us may need to be quarantined on our return. The only way any of us will be allowed near the other group is if you agree to these terms. The safety of our own people has to be our priority," he concluded bluntly.

We all nodded soberly, deep in our own thoughts, trying to decide what to do for the best.

I looked Harry in the eye. I'd known everyone in this group for some time now.

I knew that in the end everyone would say yes. Working so closely as a community over the months had pretty much beaten out any selfish traits any of us might have had. It wasn't that we wanted to take any undue risks, but if we could help others at minimal risk to ourselves, then we were more than happy to go.

As if some silent communication had taken place, Harry nodded at us all and smiled slightly.

"Thank you."

He took a deep breath and continued, "Of course there is one more possibility we have to consider. They may have been unable to respond to our calls because they're under duress. Before the plague they were a strong group, and more than capable of defending themselves and their location. If they're in a weakened state, this may have made them vulnerable to other, more hostile groups.

Therefore, on our approach, we will exercise extreme caution. I've requested a drone overflight, but due to the situation at the base, this may not be possible."

We agreed to leave at first light the following morning, to make the most of the lengthening days. Steve had asked to be included in the mission and we readily accepted his offer. It would be a good opportunity for us to work together, and for him to feel part of the group.

He was issued with a ballistic vest and webbing, and we spent the rest of the afternoon training him on basic manoeuvres and how to operate as a member of an armed team.

The training served as a reminder to us all of how far we had come together. Less than six months previously, we'd barely managed to fight off a gang when they'd tried to breach our rudimentary barricade of cars. We'd won the battle, but we'd fought naively as individuals, not as a team.

Since then, we'd been hardened by experience. Now we were a force to be reckoned with.

We had all seen combat, either in defending our homes against aggressors, or by taking action against those who had threatened to do us harm. As we ran Steve through some basic procedures to follow, based on several possible scenarios, I could see from his face that he was impressed. We all worked as a team and everyone knew their role.

He was an inexperienced shot so a lot of the training went into teaching him how to handle a gun safely. We needed to ensure that the rest of us were safe around him.

Including Steve, eight of us would be taking part in the expedition. We discussed the possibility of taking the Land Rover, but decided against it, choosing to walk instead.

By our reckoning, it would only take an hour to walk there and it would give us the opportunity to assess the area as we passed through it on the way to the warehouse. Having satisfied ourselves on the details, we retired for the night.

CHAPTER SEVENTEEN

We woke to a beautiful sunny morning. In spite of the sunshine, the early morning mist that lay across the fields like a blanket was a chilly reminder of the reason for our trip. Waving to our loved ones and friends, we disappeared into its moisture-laden embrace.

Walking in loose formation, constantly scanning the area around us for any threats, we kept the conversation to a minimum, as we walked along the route we had planned the night before.

After an hour, as we neared our destination, we tensed up slightly, all of us alert and ready to react if something happened.

Harry checked his map, and said to us in a low voice, "The main gate is on the right at the end of this run of buildings. Let me check if it's clear first and then I'll call you forward."

We watched as he jogged to the end, crouched low and looked around the corner.

Within seconds he was running back to us.

"Something's wrong", he said urgently, "the gate's wide open and I can see at least one body lying outside. Looks like gunshot wounds."

He thought for a second.

"I can't see who it is, so let's assume that hostiles have taken control. Our job now is to find out what we're dealing with."

He looked at all of us in turn, then rapidly came to a decision, "Right, apart from Steve we've all received training and taken part in operations like this. I'll take the lead, so watch for my signals. We'll use cover and advance until we can survey the site better. Then I'll assess the situation again and..."

He paused, shrugged and smiled. "Well let's just see what happens, shall we?"

Turning to Steve, he said, "Look, no disrespect, but you're not trained or ready for this. But what you can do is guard our backs. I'll point you to some cover and then I'll need you to be looking everywhere but at us. You'll need to check for anything we might have missed, and for other people approaching. And remember, never point a gun at anyone unless you're prepared to use it."

Steve nodded, looking nervous but determined.

Harry slapped him on the shoulder, "Good man. Now everyone else, you know the drill. Check your weapons and follow my lead. No heroics and remember, there could be friendlies inside the building so if you have to shoot, check your target area first. And for Christ's sake, let's put our masks on. We don't know what we're going to find."

It took us a few minutes to remove our rucksacks and make sure everyone's kit was in good order. Finally, we stood in line ready to go, the adrenaline in our systems making our hearts beat faster and our hands sweaty.

Leading the way, Harry dashed to the first cover behind a car. Using binoculars, he surveyed the area from this new angle, then using hand signals, directed us to the next point.

From my position, everything looked quiet. Nothing could be seen apart from the dead man lying in front of the warehouse.

The gates were open on the compound, which was unusual. They had been constructed by the army engineers, after the original ones had been destroyed during the attack on Gumin. They had been the first and most important means of defence the group had and they had kept them locked and guarded at all times.

Motioning for us to cover him, Harry ran to the next position. As he made for another car, a single shot rang out. The sound was deafening after the prolonged silence. Harry dived for cover, landing in an undignified heap behind the vehicle. As we sought out the gunman using the scopes on our weapons, he dusted himself off, grinned sheepishly and gave us the thumbs up to show he was OK.

No one moved for the next ten minutes.

As the moments ticked by, I realised I needed to speak to Harry but he was too far away even to hear our shouts. I would have to get closer to him. I turned to the others, "I need to get to Harry. On the count of five, fire shots into the air. *Do not* aim at the building; we don't know who's in there yet."

The others nodded, and at the first shot I was up and sprinting towards Harry. I felt something tug at my shirt just before diving for cover next to him.

As I regained my breath, Harry looked at me, "That was bloody close!" he said, pointing at my jacket.

I looked at my sleeve and was stunned to see a big hole in the fabric by my elbow. A bullet had missed me by millimetres and I hadn't even realised.

All I could think to say was, "For God's sake, don't tell Becky; she'll kill me."

Harry grinned. "Oh, the logic of love, she'll kill you for not getting shot. What would happen if you had got shot?"

"She would have killed you!" I said with a smile.

Laughing, he said, "Right, then, let's get back to solving this little problem we have."

We still couldn't see any movement, but someone was out there with a gun, and judging by my near miss, he or she was a pretty good shot.

"Oh, well," muttered Harry, "here goes nothing. We can't sit here on our arses waiting."

He cupped his hands around his mouth and shouted, "Who are you? We mean you no harm. We were just checking on our friends who live here."

A faint reply came back, "Go away, or I swear I'll kill you. Just like I killed the other ones!"

I looked at Harry. "Did that voice sound awfully young to you?"

He nodded. "It certainly did. I think we may be close to ending this."

He shouted again, "Hello, this is Harry. I've been here before. I'm here with Tom from the people in Birmingham who helped you before. If you were here at that time, then you must remember me. We played a game of football and I was in goal."

There was silence for a minute.

Hearing some noise from the warehouse, we peered cautiously out from our hiding place.

After another minute of banging and crashing, a door at the front of the warehouse slowly opened.

We raised our weapons ready.

A small figure emerged and walked slowly into view. As far as I could make out it was a boy of about eight and he was holding a rifle. It looked ridiculously large in his small hands.

We all stood up and moved into the open as he got closer. He stopped and looked at all of us, then the tension in his face seemed to melt away and he dropped the weapon and ran towards Harry.

On impulse, Harry knelt down and the boy ran straight into his open arms, sobbing into Harry's chest.

The rest of us gathered round, at a loss for words, and as the boy's sobs finally began to subside, I signalled for the others to stay sharp and keep looking outwards. We still didn't know if the danger was past.

"I remember you," Harry said softly, "you're that kid who was a great striker. I remember you scoring past me a few times."

Now I could place him. He and his sister had been orphaned when Gumin's thugs had killed their parents. After some discussion about where they should go, one of the families at the warehouse had offered to look after them, as it seemed best for them to stay among people they knew.

"Who else is with you?"

Struggling not to cry again, he said, "It's just me and my sister. Everyone else got sick. We tried to look after them, but they all died."

Harry nodded, "Where is she now?"

He jerked away as he realised he'd forgotten about her.

"She's hiding. Let me show you. When the bad men came and found us, we hid somewhere better, you'll never find her."

We still had questions, but we needed to get his sister. As we followed him, I noticed that Harry had removed his gas mask. He must have done it earlier.

A thought struck me, how had the boy recognised him?'

"Harry," I whispered, "how long have you had the mask off? You could be infected. What the hell were you thinking?"

He spoke quietly so that the boy wouldn't hear him.

"Tom, I know, but how else was he going to recognise me? I took what in my mind was a small calculated risk. But I accept the fact that I'll have to quarantine myself for a while when we get back."

I still wasn't happy with the explanation and my face must have made that plain, because he added, "Look, the boy was terrified and we needed to get that gun out of his hands before an accident happened."

He paused, then went on "And to be fair, I knew none of us would be able to shoot him, so I had to show him it was me before something unfortunate happened."

He smiled ruefully, "Kim is not going to be happy with me."

We followed the boy to the warehouse and scrambled over the remains of the barricade he'd dismantled when he came out to us. Just inside the door lay another body with dried blood pooled around it.

The stench was overpowering.

The all too familiar smell of death and corruption was like a wall we had to physically push through to continue. The boy was waiting for us to catch up.

"How can you stay in here with this smell?" I asked him, fighting down a wave of nausea. The boy seemed unmoved by it.

"We don't. There's a den on the roof. We use a ladder from the top shelf of the racking to climb up. It's safe up there. We've got enough food and I was only going to go back into the building if we ran out."

He led us into the middle of the warehouse and pointed to a rack that stretched up to the high ceiling.

"It's up there. Wait here if you want, I'll bring her here."

Diane asked, "How old is your sister?"

"Six."

She shook her head, passed her weapon to the person next to her, and started to shrug out of her tactical vest, which was weighed down with extra magazines and equipment.

"I'll come with you. She must be terrified, poor thing."

Harry did the same.

While Harry and Diane were getting ready, I asked him his name.

"Isaac," he replied solemnly. His sister, he informed me, was called Lottie, and he'd turned ten on his last birthday.

We watched as the three of them climbed the racking, using the cross supports at the racking ends like a ladder.

The boy was much more agile and kept having to wait for Diane and Harry to catch up.

Once they'd disappeared from view about thirty metres above the ground, we took a look around.

As we walked to the end of the rack, the smell of death intensified. I entered the loading bay area of the warehouse where the families and groups had constructed their main living area, with separate areas created for each family, to afford some privacy.

Every separate area was occupied by bodies covered in a variety of blankets, rugs or coats.

The entire community lay dead.

The fact that everyone had lived in such close proximity to each other had helped the disease to spread like wildfire before they'd had any idea what they were dealing with.

The children had to have been born with some natural immunity to the bacterium. It was the only possible explanation for why they had been spared.

But what they must have gone through, watching helplessly as everyone who had been close to them died a painful death, just didn't bear thinking about. And, I thought grimly, we still didn't know the story about the "the bad men" who had come yet.

On closer examination, the warehouse still contained a vast quantity of food, with pallets lining most of the racks. The shields that had been added to the racking supports had prevented the rats from climbing them and protected the food, but there had been no defence against the disease-ridden fleas they had carried.

Gumin and his men had been so efficient in scouring and emptying the surrounding area that most of the original supplies in the warehouse remained untouched.

Food was by far the most valuable currency we had now, so the contents of the warehouse would have to be moved.

Ten minutes later a sound from above drew our attention, and we watched as the two adults and two children climbed down the racking towards us.

CHAPTER EIGHTEEN

As soon as they were back on the ground, we all moved outside to escape the smell.

The two children still looked terrified. This was understandable. Aside from Harry, the rest of us were still wearing masks. We must have looked like beings from another planet.

Up close, we could see that the children were in poor condition. They were filthy from head to toe. Their tear-streaked faces were covered in grime and their hair was badly matted. They looked so small and vulnerable, standing before us and holding hands, it would have taken a very hard heart not to have softened at the sight of them.

Isaac stuck as close as possible to Harry. As we sat down, someone started to boil a kettle on a camping stove so that we could all have a hot drink. Then, as gently as possible, we managed to draw out most of their story.

The disease had spread rapidly through the tight-knit community.

Just two days after the first case, everyone had been either ill, dying or dead. Lottie and Isaac were the only ones without symptoms.

As young as they were, they had tried their best to help but they had lost everyone who mattered to them. Too young to understand or to know what to do, they had stayed on there.

They had moved to the other end of the warehouse, away from the corpses, and made a little area to live and sleep in. Isaac had done his best to look after Lottie.

Two days before our arrival, they were woken by the sound of voices. Thinking that someone was coming to help, they hurried to meet them.

The people they encountered were not rescuers. They were four men in masks, and they were searching the bodies for anything of value. Realising that something was wrong, Isaac stopped short, but before he could grab her, Lottie squeezed past him and ran right up to them.

Isaac stayed hidden and watched in horror as she was slapped, grabbed and tied up. Too young to comprehend what the men were saying they were going to do to her, but fully understanding that her life was in danger, he sprinted back to their den.

He was a smart boy and had already gathered up all the weapons the community had and put them in a safe place away from his sister. He had been scared she might hurt herself if she found one and accidentally fired it.

He had spent many hours watching the adults handle the weapons, and he knew what to do. Grabbing the one he was most familiar with, he picked up two loaded magazines. He put one in his pocket and inserted the other one into the gun and pulled the charging handle.

The sight of Isaac walking towards them, pointing a gun and shouting in his squeaky voice that they were to let his sister go momentarily shocked the three men.

Then they burst out laughing, not believing he would have the guts to pull the trigger or that he would even know how to load a gun.

But everything he had witnessed since the world had gone dark had hardened him up. He'd seen his parents murdered and witnessed the horrors Gumin had inflicted on others. The only thing he had left in his life was his sister, and he wasn't about to let anyone hurt her.

He gritted his teeth and pulled the trigger, killing the first man instantly. The recoil almost knocked him off his feet and by the time he had recovered the other three men were running full pelt for the exit.

Young as he was, he gave chase, knowing he needed to stop them, but a ten-year-old boy carrying a heavy gun could not outrun three cowardly adults, intent on saving their own skins.

Just as they reached the door, he rested the gun on a pallet of food, aimed it just as he had seen others do and pulled the trigger again.

The gun must have been on full auto because it spewed forth enough bullets to kill another of the men outright and shatter the hip of a third. The fourth man, untouched, kept running.

Once Lottie was untied, they cautiously approached the men. Two were clearly dead, but the third had managed to drag himself out of the door, leaving a trail of blood behind him as he pulled himself across the yard towards the gate.

They couldn't take him prisoner and they had neither the means nor the experience to treat his wound, but Isaac had enough humanity in him not to want to pull the trigger. As they approached the injured man, he panicked, twisting towards them and begging them to help him. The twisting must have ruptured an artery because the flow of blood increased and his cries and movements rapidly became weaker. As they watched silently, he died in front of them.

The young boy had more sense than most grown-ups. One of their attackers had escaped and he knew he could return at any time. He also knew that he was likely to bring others, and that he wouldn't be able to fight them off again.

He thought hard about what they should do. He didn't want to leave the warehouse. It was the only place he knew and he was more afraid of what was outside the fences than of what might happen if they stayed. Following Gumin's defeat, a lookout post had been constructed on the roof.

It had rarely been used, as it involved a perilous climb up racking, followed by an equally hazardous ascent up a ladder from the top of a rack, to get through an open roof light.

Undaunted, Isaac climbed up to inspect it. It was perfect.

The small but cunningly disguised lookout post had been reinforced with sandbags and gave a clear view over the front of the property.

Further back inside, a shelter had been constructed to provide protection from the elements for the sentries, who could stretch their aching backs and muscles after long periods in cramped conditions.

Despite its lack of use, it had survived the winter reasonably well and Isaac realised immediately that it would be a perfect place for him and his sister to hide.

A few hours later, he had hauled up bedding and enough food and other supplies and equipment to last them for a while. But it was only when they had pulled up the ladder and effectively "raised the drawbridge" on their castle that they felt safe.

To relieve the boredom, they spent most of the day in the lookout playing imaginary games.

When they caught sight of us the following day, they immediately thought it was the lone survivor returning with more help. Without hesitation Isaac prepared his weapon and got ready to defend their home.

The tears streamed down his face as he described his relief on recognising Harry and the realisation that their ordeal was over. The fact that he had managed, against all odds, to keep his sister safe reduced some of us to tears too.

I decided not to show him the bullet hole in my shirt and how close he had come to hitting me. This ten-year-old boy had shown more courage and determination than most adults would have done.

The harsh reality of our new lives was forcing everyone to re-evaluate the way we lived and the way we raised our children. In the past, we had cocooned our children. Death, although common in far off, war-torn countries, had been dealt with in a safe and sanitised way. Now death and all its associated horrors were unfortunately common occurrences and you could no longer shield the young ones from it. But this young boy had killed three people and was ready to kill again to protect himself and his sister.

I couldn't imagine what a psychologist would say, but it was clear that careful thought would have to be given to helping him recover.

Life was now about survival, but those of us who still valued our humanity were determined to preserve a level of common decency and mutual respect. We sincerely hoped that we would succeed.

Harry gave Isaac and Lottie a brief, "child friendly" version of what had happened to us and why we were camping out in the woods nearby. He concluded by asking gently if, providing it was OK with them, they could come and live with us from now on.

They readily agreed. I admired the way Harry handled that situation. Those children had shown a level of maturity and independence way beyond their years, by surviving for so long on their own. They had even had to kill to protect themselves and therefore they deserved to be treated as adults: capable of making their own choices.

We helped them to gather what personal possessions they had, and after securing the doors to the warehouse as best we could, we headed back to the woods.

CHAPTER NINETEEN

We had maintained contact via radio throughout the day, so the others knew that we were on our way back. We had also let them know that we would be bringing back guests who had been exposed to the disease and therefore everyone would need to wear their masks on our arrival.

Harry decided that as he had already exposed himself to risk, there was not much point in putting his mask back on.

We had all relaxed a little. Harry was carrying Lottie on his shoulders and we were walking along bunched together. The basic rule was that you had to be vigilant at all times, as danger could lurk around every corner.

But we had forgotten that.

Four of us were discussing what should be done with the food in the warehouse. The most feasible idea was for the base to mount an expedition. They had the lorries and they had forklifts, and they could transport these using low loaders.

It would take a lot of work to pull it off but the base was more than capable of handling it in terms of resources and manpower.

The twin booms of both barrels of a shotgun being fired made us all dive for the nearest cover. I looked round to see Harry lying on the floor, holding his leg and screaming and swearing in pain, Lottie, who had been on Harry's shoulders, was also screaming.

Worryingly, another of our group, Gary, was lying motionless on his back.

I had thrown myself to the ground and raising my rifle, I fired blindly in the direction I thought the shot had come from.

Everyone else followed suit. As I was changing magazines I glanced back at Harry, He was crawling painfully towards shelter, trying to keep the still screaming Lottie behind him, in an effort to shield her with his body.

A boom and the blast of shot passing close to my head forced me to roll quickly to the nearest cove behind a garden wall.

"Harry! Talk to me! Are you OK?" I yelled frantically, between bursts of rifle fire from us and booms of shotguns from our unknown attackers.

"Yes, yes. I'm OK," he shouted back. "Just got pinged by a few pellets. Hurts like hell but I don't think anything vital's been hit. Lottie's OK as well. Banged her head a bit when I fell but she's all right."

I tried to call to Gary but got no response.

Now Harry had Lottie in a safe place, he took command. He quickly established that apart from Gary, who did not look good, we were all behind cover and able to fire our weapons towards the enemy.

Our attackers had gone quiet, possibly because the sustained fire from our automatic weapons had given us fire superiority and had them ducking for cover.

Silence reigned. I thought quickly. Time to act.

"I need to check on Gary. Everyone get ready to cover me. Is that OK Harry?"

"Yes, Tom. And you showing yourself might get them to break cover."

It took me a few moments to mentally prepare myself before running into danger one more time. I closed my eyes and took a few breaths then shouted for everyone to get ready.

Then I ran as fast as I could and slid to a halt beside Gary, expecting to hear the boom and feel the pain of the shot. But it never came. Gary's face was a bloody mess. I was becoming accustomed to seeing gunshot wounds and he looked as if he'd taken the force of a heavy gauge shot gun cartridge full in the face.

Incredibly he was still alive, but barely. The range from which he had been shot must have saved his life. He was unconscious and his breathing was shallow and laboured. I felt despair. There was nothing I could do.

Part of our training had included emergency field medicine, so I knew what not to do if something like this happened.

For one thing, I knew that morphine supresses breathing and as Gary's breathing was already shallow, it would be too risky to give him any.

"He's alive but he's not good," I shouted, "I think he needs more than what we can do for him."

"Right," shouted Harry, "let's clear them out. You know the routine." With Harry directing us, the group leapfrogged forward. Harry led the way, limping badly and hopping from cover to cover.

Within five minutes it was clear that they had gone. Spent shotgun shells scattered on the ground were the only indication that anyone had been there.

After we'd checked the surrounding area to make sure they had really gone, Harry positioned everyone to provide all round security and hobbled over to where I still lay, holding Gary's hand, and talking to him in an effort to reassure him.

He took one look at Gary and the mess that had been his face. "He'll need to be evacuated to the base hospital. They're the only ones who can deal with this."

"I thought they were on lockdown because of the plague?"

"They are. The only exception is a medical emergency. And this I would say, falls into that category."

He raised Colonel Moore on the radio and put in his emergency request for a helicopter medevac.

Although the base had several working helicopters, it had been decided to restrict their use to an absolute minimum. Fuel was not a problem, but spare parts were. Routine maintenance was required after every flight and it soon became apparent that at some point in the future, the scarcity of parts would ground them. For that reason, every flight had to be authorised at the highest level to husband their limited lifespan for as long as possible.

Medical emergencies were obviously at the top of the list, so Colonel Moore lost no time in authorising the flight.

"You wouldn't be asking unless it was necessary. If one of our own needs help, the answer is yes. It should be with you in an hour," was his curt reply.

Gary couldn't be moved; we would have to wait for the helicopter and medics to arrive. We sat around feeling incredibly vulnerable. We had just been attacked and now we found ourselves in an exposed position in the middle of an urban street. Apart from the people who were trying to make Gary comfortable, everyone faced outwards, weapons held ready.

Russ spoke up, "We're sitting ducks here. Let's push some of the cars into a better position to give us all some cover."

It made perfect sense, and in no time at all, we'd broken into the nearest cars and pushed them into position so that they surrounded us.

Now that we were feeling more secure, some of us took a break behind the barricade while we rotated lookouts.

The next step was to identify the nearest landing place for the helicopter and mark it out so that it could be seen from the air. Harry sent the coordinates through to the base. Now that we had the chance to stop and think, the questions came.

"What the hell happened?" someone asked.

"We got sloppy!" I replied angrily. "That's what happened. All the things we've been through, the fights we've had, and now all that extra training we've been given means nothing. We acted like amateurs out for a Sunday stroll. We thought the mission was over and we were on our way home, and Gary paid for our mistakes."

The others listened in silence.

"Most likely the gang were returning to the warehouse," I said wearily, "Sod's law dictated we were going to meet head on. They must have heard us chattering like old women and set up a hasty ambush. The only thing they weren't expecting was all that firepower we could put down; that scared them and they ran."

"No! It was my fault," interrupted Harry, "I'm in command here; the fault lies with me and no one else. I won't have it any other way.

Yes, we messed up, but if the gang was on its way back to the warehouse, then at least we got Isaac and Lottie out in time. Dropping our guard is a mistake I will never make again, but for now we need to concentrate on getting Gary on that helicopter, and the rest of us back to the woods in one piece."

Harry raised Pete on the radio and told him what had happened. The shots had been heard up at the woods and they had been going out of their minds with worry. Harry spoke to Emma, Gary's wife, directly.

He told her what had happened and tried to be as honest as he could about the injuries he had received. He ended the call with a promise that, if possible, he would arrange for transport for her and their child, Marcie, back to the base as soon as possible.

Only then would he allow Chris to inspect his leg.

Although he had been stoically coping with the pain, it was clear that he was in a lot of discomfort. After cutting his left trouser leg and washing away the blood, Chris confirmed that the lower leg had received a good peppering. It looked bad and had bled a lot but thankfully, was mostly superficial. He gave Harry a dose of morphine, and after cleaning the wounds as best he could and applying a liberal dose of antiseptic cream to the entire area, he bandaged him up.

Once they were back in the woods he would "have a go" at removing the pellets from his leg.

The distant but unmistakable thwomp of an approaching helicopter stopped all conversation.

The helicopter looked huge as it circled above us. We could see the door gunners on either side of the aircraft scanning the area with their machine guns, ready to respond to any threat.

As soon as it touched down, four soldiers disembarked from it. Two of them moved to the front and rear of the aircraft and crouched down, presumably so that they could cover any blind spots the door gunners might have.

The other two ran towards us. Ignoring us completely, they started working on Gary. We gave them space so that they could do their job.

The noise of the helicopter and the fact that they were wearing masks made communication next to impossible. After about five minutes, and following their hand signals, we helped lift Gary on to a collapsible stretcher they had with them and two of us helped carry him to the helicopter.

As soon as he was strapped in, and after a quick handshake with the medics, the soldiers jumped aboard the helicopter and it lifted off and sped away.

The silence in the wake of the constant assault of noise from the helicopter was a relief.

Harry took command again.

"Right, let's go home. Keep Lottie and Isaac in the middle of us, keep the chat to a minimum and stay alert. We don't know where those bastards went."

Shouldering our rucksacks, we set off.

We made it back to the woods with a few hours of daylight left.

CHAPTER TWENTY

Although we were greeted with relief on our return to the camp, everyone's attention was focused on Gary's wife, Emma and his daughter Marcie, who were both distraught and desperate to be by his side.

Harry tried to comfort them by reiterating his promise of getting them to the base as soon as possible. He'd put his gas mask on before his arrival to avoid the possibility of infecting anyone.

On their arrival, Isaac and Lottie had been set apart from the main group. We'd been careful to explain this to them, and our reasons for doing so, as simply as possible and both children seemed to accept the explanation. Diane, still wearing her mask, had volunteered to stay with them, holding their hands to keep them company while they watched our emotional reunion with the others from a distance.

Harry took Kim by the hand and led her away from the group. I watched them, knowing that he was going to have to explain that he would be in isolation for a time, just in case. That was likely to be a difficult conversation.

We had talked it through earlier and he had been philosophical about it. He still maintained that the risk he had taken had been worth it. He also pointed out that someone would have to look after Isaac and Lottie, and he was now the ideal candidate for the job and that this way, there would be no danger to anyone else.

His logic was sound. Apart from the fact that he now had to tell Kim. I watched as Kim went through a variety of different emotions in a few seconds. Shock at the news, worry about what might happen to him, and anger at what he had done. Finally, to his surprise and mine, she took her revenge.

Without warning, she grabbed his gas mask and pulled it from his face, removed her own and wrapped her arms around his neck. Before he could stop her, she kissed him. I chuckled to myself and said to the world in general, "Well that's another one in isolation then!"

After Chris had worked on his leg and removed as many pellets as he could, Chris, Russ and I helped Harry move enough equipment to create a new camp for them on the other side of the woods. We figured they might as well be comfortable in their isolation, particularly as they now had two young children to look after. In the end, we had quite a pile to transport and it took a few runs to complete the operation.

After building their shelters and setting up a cooking area, we left them to it. We would be checking in on them daily (in other words, shouting to them from a distance to see if everything was OK or if they needed anything). We'd agreed on a four-day isolation period.

He had received a severe reprimand from Colonel Moore about the position in which he had placed himself. But given that it had already happened, it was taken no further.

Aware that he had got off very lightly, Harry bore the dressing-down with good grace, aware that the Colonel's fury stemmed as much from his concern about the Prince's welfare as it did from any disobedience he had shown.

The medical staff at the base were very interested in Isaac and Lottie. Other people had fallen ill and recovered from the disease, but to their knowledge, they were the first subjects to have been in prolonged and close contact with the disease and shown no ill-effects whatsoever. They had to be immune.

We knew that serious consideration had been given to whisking them off to the base for further testing, in the hope of developing a potential cure and using them as test subjects.

Thankfully, the realisation that the plague was probably burning itself out by now, and the fact that the equipment they had at their disposal would make it impossible to produce a viable vaccine in time, led to the project being shelved.

As things stood, we would have been reluctant to let them go anyway. They had suffered enough and although we could see the logic in the proposal, the thought of two traumatised children being used for medical research was something none of us were comfortable with. We were greatly relieved to hear that the plan had been dropped.

While we waited for Harry and Kim's isolation period to end, life carried on at our temporary home.

News of further deaths at home was now received with quiet acceptance. Given the appallingly high mortality rate, bad news was now to be expected. Every evening we raised a glass and shed a tear for someone who was no longer with us.

The harsh reality of the life we now led and the amount of death we had already experienced had inured us to much of the pain.

I felt blessed that none of my family had been affected. In fact, our household had been the only one to escape the disease. I had no idea why. Perhaps luck, or fate had had a hand in it. Who knows.

The day came when, except for Allan, every member of our community who'd fallen sick had died and their bodies had been disposed of. As an extra precaution, the decision was taken to burn down the house that Jerry had been using as a hospital. We all agreed that this would be the best way of wiping out any final traces of the disease. And besides, no one relished the idea of returning to a house full of ghosts and bad memories.

Jerry imposed a further week of isolation, to rule out any possibility that he or any of his exhausted carers might be carrying the bacteria. We were disappointed, but a few more days wouldn't make much difference.

The news from the base was no better. There had been no new cases since we'd last spoken, and they were cautiously optimistic about having it under control, but over fifty percent of the new arrivals had died along with a number of the original occupants. Despite this, the fact that they'd received an early warning from us meant that the death toll wasn't as catastrophic as it might have been.

The news from Balmoral couldn't have been worse. I had the sad task of informing Harry that his father had succumbed to the disease. The rescue party sent to Balmoral had arrived to find that the entire household had been wiped out. The Prince of Wales was laid to rest alongside his wife and other family members in the grounds of their Scottish estate, with as much ceremony as the small party of soldiers could manage.

Steve and his family had settled in easily and were readily accepted as part of our small community. After a few days, it felt as if they had always been with us.

The medics at the base had worked hard on Gary to remove the shotgun pellets from his face and to repair as much of the damage as possible. Despite all their efforts, he had lost an eye and his face had been left horribly scarred, but he would recover.

We had made one brief trip to the warehouse the day after we'd left, primarily to recover the weapons stored there. We didn't want to take the chance that they might fall into the wrong hands.

As far as we'd been able to tell, the men who had ambushed us had only had shotguns and we wanted to keep it that way. Had they possessed modern assault weapons when they attacked, the ending might have been rather different.

With this in mind, we had taken the Land Rover and lost no time in getting there. Once we were inside, we followed Isaac's directions to where they had been hidden, and before long we had collected every weapon we could find.

We locked the building up as best we could and closed and secured the main gate.

Back at the base, planning was now in its final stage for Colonel Moore and his team to empty the warehouse and transfer its contents back there. This was good news for Emma and her daughter, as they would be returning to the base on one of the lorries, so that they could be with Gary.

Some of Moore's staff had visited the warehouse in the past during their stay with us, so their familiarity with it made the planning relatively easy.

The proposal was quite clever and would involve exposing as few people as possible to the risk of infection.

A small contingent of soldiers would be based at the warehouse. Their initial priority would be to bury the occupants, partly out of respect but also for practical reasons.

Most of the corpses were in the loading bay and they would have to be moved to allow passage for the forklifts and lifting equipment.

The dead would be buried in a mass grave and the base chaplain would be in attendance to perform a burial service.

Every lorry and vehicle capable of carrying goods would be used to make the runs between the base and the warehouse until the contents were finally cleared. To avoid any possibility of infection, the drivers would not be permitted to leave their vehicles while they were being loaded.

It was estimated that this process would take two to three days.

As soon as Gary was well enough, he and his family would return to us once the regular vehicle runs between the base and our compound had re-commenced.

The men who had attacked were still a concern. Once the current situation had resolved itself and the remaining members of our community were together again, it would be necessary to find them and wipe them out. As things stood, we weren't in a position to mount patrols to find them, but we were careful to avoid being taken by surprise again.

The defensive positions we had built and the amount of firepower we had available to us would, ordinarily, be more than enough to protect us. But without people on lookout duty, they would be useless.

As usual, Pete managed to put together a perfect rota which gave everyone some time with their families but ensured that someone was always on the lookout.

Apart from the sadness that still weighed heavily on us for the people we had lost, that time we spent there could almost be described as a holiday. The weather was warm and the children spent whole days exploring and playing in the woods. Now that there were people constantly on lookout duty, we were happy enough to let them run free within the confines of the trees. It seemed unlikely that they would come to any harm. Saying that, when we managed to corral them up for meal times, there were always enough bruises and scrapes to send worried mothers running for the antiseptic cream and plasters.

Aside from guard duty, the adult contingent had very little to do. We had ample food and, thanks to Russ, running water.

His ingenuity never ceased to amaze us. He'd invented a very simple device that used the power of the flowing water to somehow pump it back up to us in the wood.

It did need sterilising, but as firewood was in plentiful supply this was not a problem at all.

Poor Russ. He kept trying to explain how it worked, but after about the fifth attempt we all agreed that it was magic, and if he had performed such sorcery in the Middle Ages, he would surely have been burned at the stake.

By now we had dispensed with the health checks we'd put in place, as it was clear that no one had developed any symptoms and there was no danger. When not on guard duty or carrying out the light chores necessary to keep the camp functioning, we spent the days resting and chatting around the fire, which we kept burning constantly.

Cooking had become a communal affair; more of an activity than a chore, because we all chipped in to help.

It did take a day or two to adjust to this enforced rest.

We were all used to constant activity and hard work, and just as it had always taken a few days to adapt to the pace of a summer holiday, it took us a while to get used to it. It was hard not to feel guilty about having so little to do, but we comforted ourselves with the knowledge that we'd worked virtually nonstop to survive for the past six months and there was little we could do about the current situation. We might as well enjoy it while it lasted.

Three days later Harry, Kim, Isaac and Lottie were declared free of infection and re-joined us.

We had been careful to prepare our own children and they readily and gently included them in the day's activities. Before long Isaac was tearing around with the older kids and Lottie was having the time of her life playing imaginary games with the younger ones.

Harry and Kim seemed to have thoroughly enjoyed their isolation and had clearly grown much closer.

It struck me that despite her youth and her fresh-faced prettiness, Kim had a toughness and determination that wasn't immediately apparent on meeting her. In spite of everything she had been through prior to our rescuing her, she'd won the love of a handsome, young prince. The fact that he was also kind, brave and surprisingly down to earth was an added bonus.

I smiled to myself and shook my head. In normal circumstances, the chances of their paths crossing and their falling in love would have been infinitesimal.

Fate was a strange thing.

They had formed strong bonds with Isaac and Lottie, and were adamant that they still wanted to help look after them and be involved in their lives. It came as no surprise to us to hear that the children suffered nightmares most nights. Kim could readily understand what they were going through and wanted to play a part in helping them to recover.

As the day of our departure approached, we sorted through what we planned to take with us and what we would leave.

Emma and Marcie finally received the news they had been longing for: a suitable vehicle had been made available to take them back to the base. Russ and I used the Land Rover to drop them off at the warehouse. We didn't prolong our goodbyes, because we knew we would be seeing them again as soon as Gary was fit enough to travel.

It wouldn't be possible for us to take all the food. Steve still had an enormous quantity buried at various locations around the wood, so we decided to make a careful note of them and leave them in place. He had waterproofed the storage holes to the best of his ability, so we were confident that the contents would be preserved for a good while at least.

After some discussion, we had decided to keep the campsite as a fall-back location in case we were forced to evacuate the compound again.

It made sense. It was reasonably close to home, it was familiar to us and there would be food and equipment there if we needed it. In the worst-case scenario, we could just leave everything behind and head back to the woods, knowing that we would have enough there to enable us to survive.

We gave careful consideration to the things we would leave, and how best to conceal them. Hopefully, the woods would remain undiscovered, but that could not be taken for granted, so we hid caches of camping and cooking equipment in various places around the woods.

The weapons we had collected from the warehouse were also hidden in the woods. We removed the pins from the bolt carriers and hid them in another location so that even if someone did discover them, they would still be inoperable. The ammunition was also stored separately.

Lastly, the lookout posts and defensive bunkers we had constructed were dismantled so that they couldn't be used against us if anyone else took up occupation.

If need be, it would not take long to reinstate them, and we camouflaged them as best we could in the hope that they wouldn't be obvious to anyone else.

As we left the woods early in the morning, we took a last look at the place that had been our sanctuary over the previous weeks.

We were excited to be returning home, but our emotions were mixed.

A third of the adults in our community and half of the children had died.

The community we had created and were heading back to would never be the same. We had lost so much.

But we had also made new friends.

The road stretched out in front of us, and we settled our rucksacks on to our shoulders. We let the dogs run ahead, took our children's hands and set out for home, with the much lighter Land Rover bringing up the rear.

The pace was unusually fast; an indication of our desire to return home.

CHAPTER TWENTY-ONE

The closer we got, the quieter we became.

As one, we turned the final corner and entered the road. We had been in contact by radio so they were expecting us. As soon as they saw us the gates swung open.

Jerry and Fiona were first through the gates. Sprinting towards us, they scooped Larry and Jack up in their arms and hugged them fiercely.

Emotions ran high as family members embraced. This was first time they'd all had a chance to grieve together for the loss of a parent or worse, the loss of a child.

Even Captain Berry, the "hard as nails" SAS captain, was wiping his eyes. While we had been mourning the dead at a distance, he had stayed on and witnessed the full horror of the plague, burying its victims both young and old.

It was a while before anyone felt inclined to move to the kitchen area.

When we got there the shrunken size of our community hit me forcibly. We sat down for our first meeting.

Steve, Toni and their children were introduced to everyone and made to feel welcome.

Predictably, Pete had already organised lodgings for them in a house he knew would have the space, and with people they got on with especially well.

Allan was missing from the meeting. Although he was now recovering slowly, he was still bedridden. When I saw him I understood why. His fight with the plague had clearly been a close-run thing; he seemed to have shrunk to half his size and looked pale and drawn. He sat up in bed while Michelle held his hand. She looked exhausted from the effort of caring for him.

This really brought it home to me. We had been told that Allan was doing OK and was responding to the antibiotics. If this was their version of "OK", how bad had it been for the people who had died?

The cooks soon got back into the swing of things and put together a special meal in the evening to celebrate the community becoming whole again. It also turned into a celebration of the lives we had lost, so that our last and hopefully enduring memories of them would raise some smiles as well as tears.

Before he became too drunk to speak clearly, Pete announced he would be starting the rotas again in the morning, so that we could get back to normal.

I volunteered to man one of the barricades to give some of the others a chance to let their hair down. About an hour into my shift the noise of footsteps made me turn. Harry and Paul were climbing up to join me.

"We thought we'd keep you company," said Harry, pulling his arm from behind his back and waving a bottle of whisky.

"In that case, gents…" I shifted over to make space.

Harry produced some mugs from his other pocket and poured three generous measures.

We all sat in silence as we sipped the single malt from chipped mugs, enjoying the sensation of warmth as it spread through our bodies.

"I think I know where the gang that attacked you are based," said Paul matter-of-factly.

Harry looked at him, "So that's why you called me away from Kim. You want to plan another war!"

"Well, not exactly. After you were attacked, Colonel Moore began searching for them using the UAVs. Not just for that reason. They also wanted to check on all the registered communities to see if they could find out how many had survived the plague.

An air search isn't the most accurate way of doing it, but they did find isolated pockets of survivors, so there must be more out there that we've missed. But by far the largest concentration of survivors was found just outside Alvechurch."

Harry responded by looking mystified.

"It's a small village about five miles away," I explained, "it's about halfway between here and Redditch."

Paul nodded. "They flew over them a few times to record as many images as possible because they didn't much like what they saw.

From what our analysts can work out, there's a nomadic group that seems to be travelling in a convoy of old and vintage vehicles they've managed to get working."

He pulled his tablet computer from the rucksack he was carrying and pulled up a video clip. The image was clear and showed an old Land Rover pulling into a courtyard where a number of others were parked.

I asked the obvious question.

"Why were they on foot when they attacked us then?"

"The only explanation we can come up with is that we can see no evidence of any fuel transporting capacity, so they probably scavenge it as they go and preserve it for essential travel. We suspect they patrol any area local to them on foot. The place where you were attacked and the warehouse aren't far from them at all. We also think there are more of them than can fit into vehicles, so maybe the vehicles are reserved for the group's leaders."

He paused, flicking to another picture on the screen.

"Jerry saw this and thought he recognised him, but he couldn't be sure as he'd only seen him briefly when he first arrived at the road."

I looked at the screen and gave a start.

"Rick!"

The image clearly showed a former neighbour who, along with Jim Cole, had stolen a Land Rover the day I'd first brought Jerry and his family to the road. The two men had bundled their families into the car and sped off.

Another neighbour, Ian, had tried to stop him and had been run over and killed in the process.

I stared at the still image of him, standing next to a car talking to some other men and anger welled up inside me.

"Right. Tomorrow, we go there and we kill the bastard. After what he did to us and especially to Mary, I'm going to throttle him with my own hands."

We sat quietly for a while, sipping our whisky, then Harry spoke up.

"Yes, we will, but we need to be careful. This man knows where we are, he knows we have, or at least had, supplies. The question is: why hasn't he returned yet? Has he already spied on us and seen our defences?"

"I don't know," I replied dejectedly.

"Exactly! And that's why until we do know the answers, we do nothing. Knowledge is the key, which is why we should all defer to Paul and let him come up with a plan, so we can find the answers. And THEN…" he said, nodding decisively, "we can kill the bastard."

Paul held out his glass for a top-up.

"I want to make sure everything is in order here first. A lot of things have been neglected over the past few weeks, and now that there are fewer of us, we need to make sure that we can manage everything here and cope with every eventuality. We can't expect any help from the base for at least another week, unless there's another emergency like you had with Gary, of course.

They'll be preoccupied with the recovery of the food from the warehouse and they haven't given the all-clear in terms of the plague yet.

Once all that is in order I suggest that you, me and young Harry here go for a bit of a bimble and see what we can find. Would that be all right with you? I could do with stretching my legs for a few days."

We all agreed to the plan and although they offered to stay with me, I insisted on them returning to the party. We'd spent the last weeks, and indeed the previous six months, living cheek by jowl, and sometimes the only chance to get a little time to yourself was on guard duty.

Becky and the children were already tucked up in bed, exhausted after such a long day. I managed to filter out the noise of the festivities behind me and concentrated on the road ahead, watching for any potential threat and whiling away the time by thinking and planning.

At the meeting the following morning, a few people were nursing sore heads. Pete, who was looking particularly unwell, took us all through the revised rota and the "to do" jobs list.

It was clear that with our reduced numbers things would have to change. Before the plague had hit, everyone was constantly occupied. The schedules Pete had set, although not onerous, had made efficient use of everyone's available time. Downtime or rest time had been factored in, but most people still occupied themselves during these hours with home-based activities or maintenance.

Without televisions or any of the other myriad distractions that seemed to eat up hours of our time before the event, people made the most of the daylight and spent their time doing something useful. We only got together and relaxed at the very end of the day when the darkness made most jobs impracticable.

Pete rightly decided to begin by getting everything back in order after the chaos of the previous weeks. Any patrols or non-essential expeditions outside the perimeter were put on hold. We simply didn't have enough people now that a third of our community had been lost to us. The rotas divided our duties up efficiently between restoring and maintaining security and repairing the damage caused by the rats.

We set to work re-planting all the devastated areas and hoped fervently that the weather and conditions would remain favourable, and that we had been given the right advice from the base as to what to plant. Fingers crossed, it wouldn't be long before we could begin harvesting some fresh produce.

The food provided by Chris on his foraging trips, and the fresh meat provided by the hunters, only complemented the food supplies we had stored. They certainly didn't provide enough to supplement what we had. But the fact that things seemed to be growing, reassured us that we stood a very good chance of becoming self-sufficient again.

The rabbit population hadn't suffered too badly from the rat invasion, with only a few new-born rabbits being killed. Butch and his original harem, still proudly displaying the ribbons we had used to identify them, were producing an ever-increasing colony of offspring. We had to keep reminding the younger children (and some of the people who were old enough to know better) that we weren't running a petting zoo. That cute fluffy bunny you were cuddling earlier was likely to end up in the pot.

McQueen was still taking his duties very seriously and we had several broody hens sitting on eggs. We knew it wouldn't be long before chicken would also be back on the menu.

CHAPTER TWENTY-TWO

Unsurprisingly, Becky was initially resistant to me taking part in the mission to track down Rick. Naturally, she was worried about me. But even she had to concede that I was the obvious choice to accompany them.

I knew him by sight and would also be able to identify members of his family and all the Coles who had left with him. Some of the other residents could say the same, but I was probably the fittest and best trained out of all of them.

And I really wanted to go. I knew it was my chance to get even with Rick for betraying us, and particularly for what he had done to Mary.

Becky, as usual, saw straight through me. "You're still a little boy. Even after the dangers and realities of what we've faced out there, and all the fights and battles you've been involved in, there's still that part of you that wants to go and play army with your mates, running around with your faces camouflaged, waving your big guns about."

I couldn't think of a smart reply. She'd admitted that I was the obvious choice, but as always, to cover her anxiety, she couldn't resist the chance of making fun of me.

Three days after our return to the compound, Paul, Harry and I hefted our heavy rucksacks into the back of the Land Rover. We were going to be dropped off about halfway to our destination, then we would make the rest of our way on foot. The base had been monitoring the enemy carefully, so we knew it was safe to do so.

The activity at the warehouse had attracted their attention, and a group had been spotted observing the operation from the roof of a nearby building during one of the regular UAV flyovers between the base and the warehouse.

Colonel Moore had worked with this knowledge and had slowed down the recovery operation to keep their attention on them, rather than on us at our compound.

Additional soldiers had been surreptitiously arriving on the lorries, and extra security had been set up for the others, who were told to carry on as if everything was normal.

Intelligence had confirmed that a group from the destination we were making for had been observed there on a daily basis. They were always on the same building and they kept up a constant surveillance of the activities at the warehouse. They never varied their routine. They left before dark and made no attempt to approach the warehouse.

The base admitted that it was baffling. Only a few of the men were armed with what they believed were shotguns, and they never ventured any further than the building they were observing from.

We had no idea what their motives were, but the fact that they hadn't approached the soldiers seemed significant.

In the past, when the base had first sent out the convoys to make contact with other groups, the people who had been receptive to what they had to say, had almost invariably needed help and had been grateful to encounter the first sign of any authority they'd seen since the event.

The people who had avoided direct contact, and tried to hide from the convoys were, in most cases, up to no good. OK, there were always exceptions to the rule, but in general that was what they had found.

The group in Alvechurch was unlikely to be any different. They had already attacked us without provocation, but it was likely that this initial assault had been unpremeditated.

Almost certainly they had heard our poorly disciplined, noisy approach and seized the opportunity to ambush us, beating a hasty retreat once they realised that they were outgunned.

The best guess from the "experts" was that the group lacked military, training and had come up with no better plan than to keep an eye on what was happening.

After saying goodbye to our people at the compound, Chris and Russ dropped us off at a Junction on the M42 motorway, about three miles from our destination. Taking a moment to watch them drive off, we tightened the straps on our Bergens, checked our bearings and headed off.

The chances of our being spotted were slim, but following Paul's lead we were careful to use every bit of natural cover and therefore made slow and cautious progress, before halting at a pre-determined spot from which we could get a good view of our targets.

It took us most of the day to travel the three miles and even Harry was muttering under his breath about his aching muscles and back, as we crawled the last half a mile to a small copse of trees. Paul told us (well, mainly me) that we would be following a strict no noise, no fire and minimal movement procedure when we arrived at our proposed OP (observation post).

The OP was not a disappointment. It gave us a fantastic view of the location, and some fallen trees covered in secondary growth provided excellent cover. Following Paul's hand signals, we set up and secured the position.

The plan was to continually observe and make notes of everything we saw for forty-eight hours. The duties would rotate between the three of us, with one on watch, the other keeping a check on the entire perimeter to avoid being taken by surprise and the third, resting or sleeping.

We had some extremely high-powered, low-light binoculars and a long-lens camera that could take photos or videos.

I was told that if necessary, it would also transmit images in real time via satellite back to the base. The low-light binoculars were amazing. Even with very little background light, they could turn night into day.

Food was to be eaten cold and the only leeway he gave us was allowing us to perform our "ablutions" further back in the woods, rather than into the plastic bags we'd brought with us (this was only because the location provided such good cover).

Once everything was ready, we set about our mission.

They had made their base in what I remembered had been a small country hotel. From memory (Becky and I had visited it a long time ago) it had a range of outbuildings that had been converted into additional accommodation. As a local man, Rick would probably have been familiar with the place. If I'd had to choose a good place to accommodate a large group, then this would have been the logical choice for me, too.

Six vehicles were parked in the courtyard but until they were moved, we wouldn't know if they were operational or had been there since the event.

They all looked in reasonable condition, with clean windscreens and inflated tyres, so it seemed likely that the gang members had been using them.

I studied the place through the binoculars. A few people could be seen walking around. There were a few women hanging out washing and others doing similar domestic chores, but there was very little activity at all until the light began to fade.

A group of men appeared and walked up the driveway. They were all carrying rucksacks and most were carrying a shotgun. They headed straight for a large outside table that we'd noticed earlier, which, somewhat bizarrely, had been placed in the middle of the drive just outside the front door.

Then there he was.

Rick strode out of the house, his wife by his side. My pulse quickened with rage as I watched him greet the arrivals like long lost friends. His face loomed large in my magnified vision, and I watched him smile and hold out his hands in an expansive and welcoming gesture.

I remembered that smile. Every time he had tried it on me I'd thought it was the most disingenuous thing I'd ever seen. Some of the people in the road had been fooled by it and had thought he was the best thing since sliced bread, but he'd only ever tried it on people he thought might be useful to him. He'd been a shameless social climber.

I had sussed him out early on and, being a terrible big mouth, word had soon got back to him from one of his sycophantic friends that I thought he was a bit of a prat.

From that point, he had stopped bothering with me. But by the look of it, he'd managed to work his weasel charm on this group of people. He was acting like their leader.

We watched closely as they all emptied the contents of their rucksacks on to the table. They were clearly a scavenging party offering up what they had managed to find. I imagined his grating voice as I watched him congratulate a guy who'd had some success and watched him glare disapprovingly at someone else, who clearly hadn't managed to find much.

His wife stood at his side, thin lipped, and making notes on a pad.

I thought back to when I'd known them on the road. As a couple, they'd been perfectly suited to each other. Lucy was constantly complaining about everything and reacted to what most of us would call everyday events, such as your child playing sport after school, as a potential crisis. Every time, she seemed to need a cast of thousands to help make it happen. Initially, we had helped occasionally when asked, but it hadn't taken us long to realise that it was a one-way street and our good natures were being taken for granted. At this point we distanced ourselves and let her get on with it. The last straw had been discovering that while we were looking after her son and giving him tea after school because she was so busy, she'd been going to the gym after work!

The haul on the table didn't amount to much.

As we all knew, most of the available food had already been claimed or scavenged, so if they were relying on scavenging as a way of feeding themselves, they were in trouble. No wonder they'd been watching the food warehouse so avidly. One of their number had seen its contents and they wanted it badly. They had failed twice and now they were having to sit by and watch it being emptied.

But why was Rick in charge of a group like this? Through the binoculars, I could see that the scavengers were all men and they all looked decidedly unpleasant.

He'd always been very persuasive, but how on earth had he got them to follow him?

The men split up. Some of them went into the main house and the rest headed for the accommodation in the outbuildings, at the centre of which was a courtyard.

Half an hour later, a large fire was lit in the courtyard. That attracted what must have been most of them outside again. Most of them were holding bottles and they all took turns drinking from them.

The glow from the fire made it reasonably easy for us to make out their faces in the growing gloom.

A bell rang and they all trooped into the main house for what we could only presume was mealtime. A short time later, they gathered around the fire again and continued drinking.

A few women appeared carrying more bottles and it was clear from how they were being treated that they were not loved or respected partners.

As we watched for the next half an hour, things began to make sense.

The women, who were all young and attractive, were there to serve the men and to provide for their needs. This then, was how Rick had managed to assert control. I pictured his wife hand-picking frightened and vulnerable girls, offering them food and shelter, and then drawing them into what amounted to sexual slavery. I trembled with anger. Some of them were just teenagers. It was uncomfortable to watch.

Rick appeared and was greeted by a cheer that was loud enough for us to hear from our vantage point. He was carrying another crate of bottles, and proceeded to hand them out to the men, smiling and laughing and looking (to my mind) even more repellent than normal.

The women (some of them girls really) didn't try to fight off the advances of any of the men and after another hour or so of drinking, couples were seen disappearing back to the accommodation. Finally, there were only ten men left and they continued drinking around the fire.

We noticed with satisfaction that not one guard had been posted. By two in the morning, everyone had either gone to bed or had passed out drunk by the dying fire.

CHAPTER TWENTY-THREE

Before dawn broke, Paul woke me up so that we could talk things through.

Although nothing was stirring at the house and we'd have to have been shouting for them to hear us, the three of us sat together looking outwards for any trouble, and speaking in hushed tones. Harry, who had been keeping watch while I slept, spoke first.

"That's the biggest bunch of idiots I've ever seen down there. I don't know how they've got this far!" he whispered incredulously. "They've got no sentries, no discipline and absolutely no respect. I don't know what that Rick's told them, but if they're willing to act as his muscle, he must have spun them a hell of a yarn. And as for how they're treating the women, it's as bad as anything we've seen or heard of."

His voice hardened as his fury built, "I don't know about you, but I'm for going down there now and taking them all out while they're sleeping! Why do people act like this? Some of those girls down there must be underage.

I know something like this can bring out the worst in people, but there just doesn't seem to be any middle ground; either you pitch in to try to make the best of the situation – be willing to help others and contribute to building something new, or you use what's happened as an excuse to be a complete bastard and take exactly what you like from whomever you want, and to hell with the consequences."

He shook his head, "As far as I'm concerned those men down there fall into the second category and they deserve what's coming to them."

Paul and I exchanged glances, then nodded in agreement.

Paul, speaking softly, replied, "I'm with you there, Harry, but we can't storm in there like Judge Dredd dispensing justice. There are too many of them. We're better trained and better armed than they are, but if it's just the three of us, I can't guarantee success.

If just one of them took us by surprise, we'd be in serious trouble.

I suggest we continue our surveillance today as planned, and get an accurate idea of their numbers, habits and routines. Then we can come up with a plan to deal with the bastards!"

Harry, tired from his long shift, yawned and bedded down in the back of the OP, while Paul and I continued watching. A gentle kick every now and then stopped his snores from getting too loud.

After the drinking of the night before, we weren't expecting them to be early risers and they didn't disappoint. It was after ten before two groups left. We presumed that one group had been despatched to keep an eye on the soldiers at the warehouse and that the others, who were all carrying rucksacks, were going scavenging.

Of the groups that had left, we counted twenty men in total.

After another hour of careful scrutiny, the only other men we observed were Rick and two others.

As these were by far the largest and roughest looking of all the men we had seen, I imagined that Rick, typically, had made them his lieutenants and given them extra privileges to keep their loyalty.

Once we'd satisfied ourselves that including Rick, there were no more than twenty-three men, we concentrated on finding out about the women.

They were coming in and out of the house and they all seemed to have their allocated tasks. As before, none of them gave the appearance of being under duress and the men paid them little attention. It seemed to me that they could easily have made a break for it if they'd wanted to, but something seemed to be stopping them.

I was mystified. There had been no signs of any children, so they clearly weren't staying for that reason. I was roused from my thoughts by Paul hissing at me to get my attention.

He'd been on main watching duty while I was scanning the perimeter. I turned my binoculars in the direction he was looking.

Two of the women had left the buildings and were heading straight towards us. They seemed in no particular hurry, and from time to time they would stop to look at a book one of them was carrying, or to uproot a plant or pick leaves from it, placing it carefully in a basket.

Paul spoke softly, "They're foraging for food. Sod's law they'll walk right into us. Give Harry a kick; we'll all need to be awake for this."

Seconds later Harry was wide awake and alert. A few hand signals from Paul told him everything he needed to know. The OP had been well camouflaged with natural vegetation from our surroundings and netting we had brought with us, so we were confident that unless they literally fell into our laps, they wouldn't know we were there.

They stopped about twenty metres away from us, and we found we could make out snatches of their conversation. They were still looking at the book and they were laughing together about whether to add a poisonous plant or two to their collection.

One of them, still smiling, nodded in our general direction.

"Let's see if we can find enough mushrooms from under one of those fallen trees over there to finish them all off. And anyway, I need a sit down and we're too far away for Rick the Prick to nag us. Come on."

To our alarm, she pointed towards the very trees we were crouching behind.

We looked at each other and sank lower.

The women settled themselves on the log within touching distance.

I tried to be as still and quiet as possible.

Every breath I expelled sounded to me like the roar of a bellows and every slight movement I made seemed to make a rustling noise. How could they possibly not hear me?

But they seemed oblivious to any noises and carried on talking. The more we heard, the more we understood about their situation. One of the women was comforting the other, because she'd been beaten by one of the men for refusing to do something particularly degrading.

"Since we left the other group, they're getting worse. They seem to think they can do what they want to us. We put up with this all winter, because the alternative meant being thrown out and starving or freezing to death. But I don't think I can take any more. I'd rather risk it out here on my own."

There was a pause while her friend digested what she'd said, then she spoke up.

"Look, I know what you're saying, but we'll just be taken by another gang eventually. We've seen it happen. I know it's getting worse here, but at least we know them and what to expect from them. We know the ones who are a bit softer and won't be too violent towards us.

There's nothing we can do. We'll just have to put up with it and try to protect the younger ones as much as we can. We think it's bad for us, but for them it must be really awful. At least we can rationalise what's happening to us."

"Look at Penny!" replied the first woman. "She's just fourteen! She shouldn't have to go through anything like that.

When I was her age all I had to worry about was my school work and the boys I had a crush on. That creep Mike's got his eye on her you know. I've been trying to keep his mind off her, but I don't think it's going to work for much longer. The guy's a pyscho!"

"Oh my God! So that's why you've been going off with him every night?" There was a pause, and some snuffling and I visualised the first speaker nodding and trying not to show that she was upset.

"Why didn't you say?" said her friend. "We would have helped."

The other woman cleared her throat, as if she was trying hard to pull herself together, but when she spoke her voice was shaky, as if she was still close to tears.

"No. It's my job. I can't ask any of you to do it. That just wouldn't be fair. I promised Penny I'd look after her. I can cope with Mike; she won't be able to. You all do your bit to protect her, but lately he's been getting really nasty … look, I don't want to go into details but that's why he hit me, because I wouldn't do what he wanted last night.

But you know what? He's a cowardly little worm at heart. Once he'd knocked seven bells out of me to prove he was the boss, he didn't push me again to do what he wanted."

Her voice tightened with anxiety, "Penny won't be able to refuse. I'm frightened he'll kill her if he acts out one of those sick fantasies of his." She paused, and this time the other woman could think of nothing to say in response. Finally, the first woman spoke again, "It's how I rationalise it, you see. I'm doing it to protect her, so what I'm doing is right."

She broke down in tears.

I moved my head slightly. I could see the two women hugging each other for comfort.

I was deeply depressed by what I'd heard. The women here had obviously been left with no choice but to resort to the oldest trade in the world to ensure their own survival. But they were still clinging on to their sense of pride and had enough kindness and humanity in them to want to protect the more vulnerable girls in their group.

It took several minutes for the first woman to calm down and then the conversation resumed.

Paul nudged Harry, and I recognised their hand signals. Paul wanted to grab them and haul them into the OP.

It was a risky thing to do, but we were some distance from the hotel so it seemed unlikely that anyone there would hear or see anything.

Paul held up his fingers and silently counted down to three.

On one, Paul and Harry jumped up and in one smooth movement, clapped their hands over the mouths of the women and dragged them backwards into the shelter.

Their muffled screams and wide fearful eyes showing their shock at the sudden change in their circumstances.

I got to my knees ready to help.

The woman Paul had grabbed suddenly arched her body, and taking him by surprise, wriggled out of his grip.

Twisting round abruptly, she kneed him firmly in the groin and as he rolled away in agony, locked his head in a vice-like grip while landing blow after blow on him with her flailing legs.

I didn't know what to do.

Paul, highly trained in all forms of self-defence and unarmed combat, had been bested by this woman in the space of a few seconds, and was now in danger of being throttled to death.

His face was changing from red to purple, as each kick from her legs forced more of the remaining air from his lungs.

I looked over at Harry. In stark contrast, the woman he was holding seemed to have frozen in terror. His hand was still clamped over her mouth but she was making no effort to free herself. She seemed to be hypnotised by the sight of her friend, who was still managing to maintain her choke-hold on Paul.

Pulling my Glock from its holster, I pointed it at the woman and said as loudly as I dared, "Stop it! We're here to help you!"

The first woman glanced at me but barely seemed to register what I'd said and made no move to release Paul, who appeared to be losing consciousness.

Knowing that the gun's safety was on, I leaned forward and pointed the gun at her head.

"Stop it!" I said, loudly this time. "We want to help you."

This time she looked at me properly, and for the first time she seemed to take in her surroundings. She stopped kicking Paul, but kept her arm around his throat.

Still pointing my gun at her, I said softly, "Do you think you could let my friend breathe now? He's gone a very nasty colour. I know it may not look that way, but we really are here to help you."

I looked over at the woman Harry was still restraining.

"We still need you to be quiet, so if Harry takes his hand away from your mouth, will you promise not to scream?"

She nodded, her eyes still frightened. I looked at the other woman.

"And you, Boudicca! If I put my gun away, do you promise not to beat up the SAS captain anymore?"

Harry couldn't help but smile at my comment and some of the tension seemed to dissipate a little.

She nodded and released the pressure on Paul's throat. Paul was incapable of doing anything but roll away and gasp for breath.

Harry released the other woman and she immediately crawled to the other one. They held each other for support.

We sat in silence for a full minute while we all calmed down.

Paul's attacker spoke first, her voice harsh and suspicious.

"Who are you, and where the hell have you come from?"

I looked at Harry, who merely nodded for me to respond.

"We came here because of Rick," I explained. "I've got a personal score to settle with him."

She looked at me, as if weighing me up, "How do you know Rick? Did you work with him for the government?"

The shock on my face was clear to see.

"Government? Look, I don't know what he's been telling you all, but he worked in insurance! Some boring job. I could never be bothered to pay any attention to him when he was trying to tell me how important he was."

She shook her head emphatically. "No! He worked for the government. He knew exactly what had happened and what cars to get working.

He helped to form the group and protect us from the rogue government forces that were trying to take control."

I shook my head in disbelief. "I can assure you everything he knows, he learned from someone else - mainly me by the sound of it. But we haven't got time for that now. Will you be missed if you don't get back soon?"

"I doubt it. We're running out of food, so his bitch of a wife gave us a book on foraging and a basket each and told us not to come back until they were full. She does nothing herself. We have to look after her and her two brats like they're royalty."

The women had calmed down enough to pay more attention to us. It was obvious that they recognised Harry, but couldn't quite take in the fact that it was him. I remembered how surreal it had felt for me on first meeting him.

I broke the ice by introducing us and confirming that, yes, it was Prince Harry they were staring at.

Mel and Louise were both blonde and good looking and I reflected wryly that Rick had always had an eye for the pretty women in our road (Becky had been no exception, although she'd always made it patently clear that she was unimpressed by him). Mel was the taller of the two, with a swimmer's build (her strength had taken Paul by surprise, after all).

Her cheekbone showed some recent bruising and her lip was split and slightly swollen. She was clearly the one who'd fallen foul of Mike the previous night.

Louise was small and delicate. No wonder Harry had been able to subdue her so easily. I guessed that she was no more than eight stone and she looked about five foot three.

Once they'd recovered from the shock of encountering Harry, I gave them a quick summary of who we were, where we had come from and what had been happening countrywide.

Then came their story.

They had been with the group since just before the snows had set in, but had been told about its origins by the other women.

After leaving the road, Rick had quickly made alliances and formed a larger group, assuming control by claiming that he had been a senior government minister, who had managed to escape after the army had taken control.

He was a gifted storyteller and his story seemed plausible enough. Most of the people he had encountered had been hungry and confused and Rick, with his working car and his air of authority and assurance, had inspired enough confidence for people to want to follow him.

He had assured them that once order was restored, he would be welcomed back and would assume his rightful place, in the seat of power.

By association of course, those who had helped him along the way and remained loyal to him, would be treated as heroes.

Until that time, he had no choice but to hide from the army, who had staged a coup and formed a military dictatorship.

Bizarre as that might sound, Rick could be very plausible. And these were desperate people.

Using an army of thugs, Rick had organised raids to "liberate supplies" from weaker groups in the area and had hit the jackpot when a small convoy of lorries was discovered, abandoned but still full of food, on a road in the middle of nowhere.

He had set himself up like a despotic emperor in a large country house in a remote part of Devon. Using the stolen Land Rover, they had sought out similar vehicles and played the part of the "government in hiding".

Only the toughest, most violent men passed his "interviews" and were permitted to join the group, and it was an open secret (no doubt broadcast by Rick) that those who failed to pass were executed on the spot by his lieutenants. This, it was explained, was in the name of national security, to safeguard the secrecy of his location.

Fear kept everyone in line.

The men who were allowed to join him were all "believers" who could be manipulated through the web of lies he spun.

The women who were found, or who approached the group for help, were initially vetted by Rick's wife, but the final say-so came from Rick. They were permitted to join if they fulfilled a set of criteria.

They had to be young and attractive to the men.

Children were not allowed; they were extra mouths to feed and a waste of valuable resources. They were also a distraction.

Every woman was clearly told what was expected of them. They were there for the men's enjoyment and there were domestic chores to be carried out. If they refused on either count, they would be thrown out into the cold. If they agreed, they would receive food and shelter.

It was as simple as that.

Louise broke down at this point. She explained that not a day went by when they didn't feel ashamed of what they had settled for. And yet the only other option had been starving to death.

Harry spoke softly to them.

"No one will ever think that of you. The world's changed and it's brought out the very worst in people. We've seen some truly deplorable human behaviour. But what you did – well you needed to do it to survive and that's all there is to it.

When we get you out of here, no one will judge you or make you feel ashamed about what you had to do. There's nothing to be ashamed of. My own girlfriend, Kim, was in a similar situation before we rescued her. We'll help you. It's those bastards down there that are in the wrong, not you."

Louise managed a smile, and Mel continued with their story.

Everything had changed when the plague had come. As soon as the first person had fallen ill, Rick had panicked. It had broken out first in one of the converted barns on the country estate they had taken over. The barns had been some distance away from the main house, so the infection hadn't spread to begin with.

But Rick had comprehended the seriousness of the situation straightaway. He'd ordered an immediate evacuation. All the working vehicles had been loaded up with supplies, and he'd left everyone behind who'd had any contact with the disease.

The result was that most of the people in the community he had formed were left behind, and abandoned to their fates, while Rick, his family, his most trusted bodyguards and some of the women, had fled back to the Midlands.

I shook my head. Another example of Rick's twisted moral compass.

I explained at this point, that although Rick had acted selfishly and thought only of saving himself, he had almost certainly saved all their lives.

Along the way, they had encountered other groups who had been struck by the plague, and Rick had soon realised the necessity of keeping as far away from humanity as possible. After a week of travelling along back roads, Rick had led them to the hotel they were currently occupying. He'd made sure of his men's loyalty by promising them that he knew of a location in Birmingham that had food and more women for the taking.

He obviously meant us.

Paul, who by now had recovered enough to speak, or at least croak, asked them for details about the quantity and types of weapons they had. We were relieved to learn that our count had only been out by one and that as we'd suspected, all they had was shotguns.

Paul looked at the nearly empty baskets at their feet. (I'd hastily retrieved them in case anyone saw them abandoned and raised the alarm).

"We can't have you going back empty-handed. I'll fill these up for you and put some finishing touches to the plan I've got in mind. Could you bear with me for a few minutes, please, ladies?"

We all watched, while he grabbed the baskets and slid out of the back of the OP then half crawled out of sight into the woods.

Mel and Louise were full of questions and while we waited for Paul to return, we did our best to answer them all.

They were filled with elation at the thought that their ordeal might soon be over and they talked non-stop about how good it would be to feel safe again. They could scarcely believe that there were still some good people out there, people who wanted to help and not just take what others had.

Twenty minutes later Paul crawled back into the OP with the two baskets, which were now overflowing with leaves, berries and mushrooms.

"I want you two to take these back to the house and then tell whoever's down there that there's loads more, and that you need to come back again. I've got a few radio calls to make before I can finalise the plan, but we'll need your help to make this work. Do you think you can do that?"

Louise nodded. "When Lucy sees all this I'm sure she'll send us back. As I said, we're almost out of food now and the scavenging parties aren't finding much. Rick was relying on that warehouse he found and was livid when your army guys got there first.

The only thing they have got plenty of is booze. He found a storeroom full of it in the hotel and he's stopping everyone from moaning about the lack of food by letting them get drunk every night. That's why they've all been so volatile lately.

Lucy keeps a list of who collected the most food and rewards them with first choice of one of us. More often than not we have to go with more than one of them a night. If we don't, Mike beats us and Lucy holds back our food allocation. It's how he keeps them all following him."

Mel picked up her basket, wiping her eyes.

"Thank you, we'll be back as soon as we can."

She looked at Paul.

"I'm sorry I hurt you, I didn't know I could do that. I only ever went to one self-defence class."

He looked at her, and to my amusement, turned red with embarrassment.

"I'm glad you didn't go to the second one," he said, still sounding somewhat hoarse.

On impulse, she stepped forward and kissed him on the cheek.

As we watched them walk back to the hotel, I looked at Paul. He was staring after them with a strange expression on his face.

"Are you OK, mate?" I asked.

He blinked once, looked at us both and whispered, "I think I've found the woman I want to marry!"

Anyone passing by at that moment would have been deeply suspicious of the stifled snorts of laughter emanating from the vegetation.

CHAPTER TWENTY-FOUR

Paul gave us a brief outline of the plan he had come up with. More than thirty soldiers were now at the warehouse, either guarding it or helping to move the supplies. Once Rick's observation party had set out back to the hotel, he hoped to get permission for about twenty of the soldiers, led by the detachment of SAS that had been sent to reinforce the defences, to make their way to our location in the woods.

If Mel and Louise agreed, he wanted them to get everyone as drunk as possible. Once they were either asleep or too drunk to matter, he would lead the attack. If it was done correctly, hopefully everyone would be bound and gagged before they knew what was happening to them.

Once again, a simple plan that, fingers crossed, should have a high chance of success.

Taking the radio to the far side of the woods to avoid being overheard from the hotel, he went to put his plan to Colonel Moore. Harry and I focused our binoculars on our objectives. We watched as Mel and Louise walked into the house carrying their baskets.

Twenty minutes later they re-emerged carrying empty baskets. This time they were accompanied by a young girl, also carrying a basket. The girl was walking between them, chatting happily and holding Mel's hand.

Harry whispered, "Ten to one that's the young girl Penny they were talking about earlier."

"Not arguing with you there. I wonder why they're bringing her as well."

"Well, we'll find out soon enough."

They made their way slowly up the hill towards us, keeping up the pretence of foraging by occasionally stooping down to pick up a plant. I was impressed by how well they managed to disguise their approach.

About halfway up the hill to us, Mel stopped, crouched down next to the young girl and began to talk rapidly to her.

"They must be telling her about us."

"Good," I replied, "We don't want her screaming blue murder when she sees us."

As Mel spoke to her, the girl involuntarily jerked her head and looked in our direction. Mel used her hand to gently turn her head and we guessed that she was warning her not to give away our position. They continued up the hill, carefully avoiding the OP, and entered the woods about fifty yards away from us. Five minutes later they crawled into our position. The young girl was wide-eyed with amazement.

"This is Penny," said Mel, smiling.

"Are you coming to rescue us?" she asked in a sweet voice.

I answered gently, "Yes we are. We're going to take you somewhere safe. You'll have plenty of food and there'll be kids your own age you can play with." She burst into tears, threw herself at me and hugged me.

"Thank you! Thank you! I don't like it here. I've been so scared," she said, over and over.

Mel stroked her hair. "I had to bring her. Mike's really getting out of hand and I can't leave her on her own with him. He's already started drinking and I found him trying to touch her. Louise told him to stop it and he backhanded her." For the first time, I noticed a red mark on the side of Louise's face. She hadn't had it earlier.

"I told Lucy I needed her to help me gather more food and got her out of there before Mike could say anything."

"Who is this Mike?" Harry asked.

She curled her lip in disgust. "He's Rick's right-hand man. He's vicious. I think he used to belong to one of those right-wing neo-Nazi groups. He's not all that bright, but Rick likes him because he agrees with everything he says and will do whatever he wants, no matter how horrible it is. He's the biggest, strongest bloke in there, so no one'll stand up to him."

"Don't worry about that," Harry said, his voice cold, "I don't think he'll be around for much longer."

A small noise and a low hiss warned us of Paul's imminent arrival. He slid into the OP, smiled at Penny then glanced at Mel and went bright red.

"It's all agreed. Reinforcements from the warehouse will arrive tonight and once we're in place, the plan will be executed." He looked at Mel and Louise.

"That's if you two ladies are able to assist us, of course."

They spoke in unison, "We'll do anything to get away from here."

Paul outlined the plan for them and without hesitation they agreed to help.

Louise said grimly, "I'll endure one more night of hell with those bastards if it means there'll be an end to it. Trust me, I'll get them all drunk and happy and give them a night they won't forget. Just make them pay for what they've done." She paused, then looked at us, "What will you do to them when you capture them?"

Harry told them about the rules we were trying to run the country by, and what happened to those who breached them.

She looked pensive. "I thought I'd never say this but, I don't care if you hang them all from the nearest tree. No one should make another person suffer like they have us.

We're human beings but they've treated us like commodities. There's no compassion, no respect and no love in this place. It's all about power and control and cruelty.

I had a boyfriend before all this happened. We really loved each other. They killed him while one of them was raping me. They're so stupid. It's as if they think I've somehow forgotten! Every time one of them touches me or makes me have sex with him, I let them. I just try to imagine being somewhere else …" she tailed off and her eyes filled with tears.

"I always knew I'd get my revenge and now you can make it happen. They didn't have to do what they've done. They controlled the food and they had the power. They're a bunch of sadists."

Harry took her hand and squeezed it. "You're one brave woman, Louise. Given time, you'll heal, I can guarantee that. Wherever you decide to go after this, you'll find good people who'll want to help you."

Mel looked at Paul. "We'd better be getting back soon. Lucy told us not to be too long, because they'll need what we can find to feed everyone. Could you help me fill the baskets?" Paul nodded awkwardly, and the two of them slid out of the shelter together. While we were waiting for them to return, an idea occurred to me.

"Louise, do you think Penny could stay here with us? Would she be missed if she didn't go back? It's just that even though nothing should go wrong, we can't guarantee that. I think it would be safer for her if she could stay here."

"I was just thinking that myself," she replied, frowning. "I'm sure we could manage it; it's a big house, so we could just keep making up excuses about her being in another room or another part of the house. No one pays her much attention apart from Mike, so I'll just have to help Mel keep him distracted."

I knew the implications of what she was suggesting, and was touched by her courage. On impulse, I reached out and squeezed her shoulder in a pathetic attempt to offer some support. She smiled and shrugged her shoulders.

To begin with, Penny wasn't at all happy about being left behind with us, but drawing on the extensive experience I'd gained from raising my own children, I managed to win her trust and she agreed to stay.

In other words, I bribed her with sweets and chocolate.

By the time Mel and Paul had returned with three full baskets of foraged food, Penny was happily chatting to Louise and me and was positively brimming over with excitement about staying in the OP and waiting for more soldiers to arrive. The three baskets were loaded with leaves, berries, mushrooms and roots. Paul gave them both their final instructions.

Firstly, they agreed not to tell any of the other women what was happening. It would only take one wrong comment or some odd behaviour for suspicions to be aroused.

Secondly, he asked them to do their best to disable or at the very least hide, as many of the shotguns and cartridges as they could. The fewer they had available to them, the better.

He then spent several minutes describing the best way to disable a shotgun (by separating the barrel and the stock).

If everything went to plan, the attack would begin at around four in the morning. This was complicated by the fact that neither of them possessed a watch. Unhesitatingly, Paul took off his wristwatch and handed it to Mel saying,

"Look after it please; it belonged to my father."

Harry removed his, gave it to Louise and said with a smile, "Look after that one too; it was my great grandfather's!"

Paul threw him a look of mock disgust and whispered, "Bloody show off."

Louise, who looked positively horrified at the thought of holding a priceless antique watch that had belonged to King George VI, immediately thrust it back at Harry. He shook his head and grinned, telling her that it had survived a number of scrapes during its long life, so one more wouldn't matter.

We wished them luck and watched as they exited the OP and took a more circuitous route back to the hotel, in the hope that no one would notice one of them being missing.

We settled back down to continue our surveillance and wait for the reinforcements to arrive and during that time, we got to know Penny a little better. She was from Bristol and her story had a familiar ring.

When the event had happened, her parents had opted to stay at home until the food had run out, hoping and trusting that the government would soon have everything working again. Once the food had gone, and with it, any hope of help arriving, they had joined the growing throng of refugees leaving the city. They had sought shelter at an army-run refugee camp, and experienced worsening conditions and the breakdown of society that was happening at every level.

The distributed rations had become smaller and smaller until finally a fight had broken out, and an attempt had been made to take control of the food supplies by force. The soldiers had opened fire and hundreds of people had been killed in the ensuing chaos. The camp had fallen apart after that and in spite of the approaching winter, and the lack of food and shelter, most people had been forced to move on.

Penny and her parents had managed to find shelter in an old, dilapidated barn in a remote part of the countryside. Slowly starving to death, they tried their best to scavenge what food they could find. In desperation, Penny's father wandered further each day, battling his way through the freezing weather until one day, he didn't return.

Penny wept as she described how she and her mother had huddled together helplessly, waiting for him to come back. After about a week, they decided to set out and look for him. They knew they would die if they stayed and if they found him, hopefully they might also find somewhere better.

For two days, they walked and walked, desperate to find any traces of him.

Finally, they stumbled down a lane, soaked to the skin and weak from lack of food, and were surprised to see a Land Rover appearing around a bend.

The Land Rover headed straight towards them and then slowed down to a halt. For a moment, their hopes were raised, but then Mike stepped out of the car and stood there, staring at them.

Penny's mother sensed immediately that they were in danger and grabbed her daughter by the arm. They tried to make a break for it across a field, but they were both malnourished and exhausted. Mike and his men had no trouble catching up with them.

Mike took one look at her mother and said, "This one's too old." Then he nodded at Penny, "Bring her. I like them young. If we feed her up a bit, she'll be right up my street."

As Penny was bundled into the back of the car, her ears filled with her mother's screams, and she knew she was desperately fighting to get to her daughter.

The men laughed and taunted the poor woman, as she tried to push through them to reach her. Then she raked her fingers down Mike's cheek and drew blood, and he yelled in pain.

As Penny looked on helplessly, Mike had taken a baseball bat out of the car and beaten her mother to death. Screaming obscenities at her as she lay dying, her movements getting weaker by the second, he continued to rain blows down on her as her blood stained the snow around her crimson. Even after she was dead, he continued for some minutes, spittle running down his chin in his rage.

Penny had been brought back shivering and paralysed with shock and terror. Mike had pushed her towards Mel with instructions to feed her up, stop her crying and to let him know when she was ready for him.

Harry and I sat there, unable to speak. I thought about my own daughter. And I thought about what I would like to do to Mike.

From the very first day, all the women had gone out of their way to be kind to her. Apart from Lucy of course.

She knew about sex and she knew what Mike wanted to do to her, and of course she was terrified.

It was clear from what she said, that in spite of everything they were going through, Penny's arrival had given the older women a sense of purpose. It was almost as if she became a kind of mascot for them. If they could save one poor innocent girl, then it made their own suffering a little easier to bear.

She told us how Mel was constantly steering Mike's attention away from her, doing everything she could to delay the moment when he decided he would take her. Penny had known that day would come soon and had sensed his growing impatience. The tears streamed down her face and she thanked us over and over for saving her.

When she was a little calmer, we tried to change the subject to more cheerful topics. In spite of the trauma she had been through, she was sweet and funny and the time passed quickly as we talked quietly and kept watch. In between noting the arrival of the various groups, as dusk began to fall, we told her funny stories about the road occupants she would soon be meeting.

From Mel and Louise, we knew precisely how many men were at the hotel, so we were able to account for all of them as they arrived.

Once they were all present, the same routine took place as before.

The loot was handed over for Rick to inspect, and Lucy noted everything down in her book. Then everyone dispersed back to their quarters. We made a careful note of where each of them went.

Paul had made a sketch of the target building and taken notes of everyone's locations. Hopefully this would give us an advantage when we entered the site.

The soldiers who were due to arrive would not have seen the building in daylight hours, and therefore they would be wholly reliant on Paul's hand-drawn plan to get up to speed on the mission.

As before, pallets were stacked and soon the fire was blazing away.

Mel and Louise were playing their parts. We watched as they kept bringing out more bottles and we could see from their gestures that they were encouraging them all to drink up.

Few men need much encouragement to drink up. Had they been a little more sober, they might have wondered why the women were given them so much attention, but alcohol slows down the brain as well as reactions, and they lapped it all up. When the dinner bell sounded, the cheer could be heard from our OP. As we watched them troop into the building, Paul held his hand to the headset in his ear, in the universal "I'm receiving a message" signal.

Looking at us he said, "They're at the edge of the wood, I'll go and guide them in."

He slipped out of the rear of the OP and disappeared silently into the night.

CHAPTER TWENTY-FIVE

Before long, we heard footsteps approaching, crunching and crackling through the woods. Noise travels well at night, but we were confident our quarry wouldn't hear anything.

Paul crawled in, closely followed by a second man.

"Can I introduce you to Captain Digby? He's leading the SAS detachment and is in overall command of all the men who have arrived."

"Diggers! How the devil are you?" interrupted Harry.

"Oh! Sorry. I forgot you two know each other. It's been a while since we were at the base together. In fact, it seems like a lifetime ago."

Captain Digby saluted Harry and then shook hands with us both.

Paul continued.

"You two keep watch, and I'll take Captain Digby and his men to the other side of the wood. I'll talk them through the mission and show them all the plan of the site I've drawn up. Then we'll come back and give everyone the chance to get their eyes on the target."

As Harry and I were both in agreement with this, they left the OP without delay. Soon after, quiet voices and footsteps could be heard, receding into the distance.

Sudden movement at the hotel drew our attention. Mealtime was clearly over because men were drifting out to sit around the fire.

The party mood was still prevailing and they were all continually swigging from bottles. As before, Louise and Mel were valiantly laughing with them, and handing them fresh bottles as soon as the empty ones were tossed into the fire.

The good news was: all twenty-three men appeared to be present. Even Rick appeared briefly, bringing more bottles with him, and handing them out like a benevolent leader.

I pictured him congratulating himself, thinking that the atmosphere was down to his excellent leadership skills and the loyalty the men felt for him.

I watched as he moved among them, playing the genial host. One man walked beside him, his huge, powerful frame and his whole demeanour making him look every inch the bodyguard.

"That must be Mike," I whispered. Again, I was impressed by Mel's courage. He looked as if he could snap her in two.

Turning to Penny, I asked her to look through the binoculars and confirm who he was.

She looked through, turned a little pale and nodded. It was him.

We all watched as he stuck close to Rick, who was weaving his way like a snake through the drinking men.

By now most of them were well on the way to being drunk, and the women were receiving increasingly amorous attention.

I knew Mel and Louise would have kept their promise not to tell the other women, but the others seemed to have picked up on their mood all the same, and they were all working hard to keep the men happy, allowing themselves to be grabbed and fondled while they handed out more bottles.

Mike matched the description we'd been given perfectly. He stood a good six inches taller than everyone else and his bulging muscles stretched the arms of his coat.

Harry whistled, "He's a big boy, I think we should let Paul deal with him," he said, half-jokingly.

Penny spoke up, her voice small and trembling.

"This is when he usually lets them know who's getting first choice out of the women. Normally it's the one who's collected the most food. We dread this part. Apparently, some of them are OK, but there are some really psychos among them. They know they can't get out of it, but they work hard to be picked by the ones who are at least nice to them."

Harry and I exchanged furious glances. Rick was just unbelievable: there was no sense of humanity in him and he clearly just used people like pawns to maintain control.

Harry went back to looking through the binoculars and muttered quietly through gritted teeth, "That's right, you bastards. Just enjoy yourselves while you can. I don't think tomorrow's going to end well for you."

Paul and Captain Digby squeezed back into the OP.

"Right, guys," said Paul briskly, "Diggers is fully up to speed with the plan. Everyone's going to spend the next few hours getting eyes on the target and familiarising themselves with layouts and faces. Diggers and I will target each individual and allocate them to a team to take down."

He looked at Penny. "We think we've got a reasonable idea of the layout, but would it be OK if we asked you a few questions?" She nodded, eager to help, and he smiled at her.

"Once everyone is 'mission ready' they'll grab some kip in shifts until zero hour."

He glanced down to look at his watch and frowned momentarily, before recalling that he hadn't lost it, but had given it to Mel.

"Anyway," he continued, "we're aiming to go at 0400 hours and be ready to execute at 0415 hours. There'll be more of us than there will be targets, so I'll overlap the men on the individuals we identify as being likely to give us the most trouble."

He looked at Penny.

"I want you to help me with that by telling me who the most likely candidates are."

"Yes, I can do that," she said firmly, "I know which ones the others are most afraid of."

Penny spent the next half an hour, lying sandwiched between Paul and Captain Digby, identifying each of the men and helping them understand who was who.

She also helped to identify where the men usually slept and before long, Paul's hand-drawn target plan was covered in notes, circles and lines, all filled in under the dim glow of a shielded, red-lensed torch.

Most of the men had their quarters in the rooms off the courtyard. It was easy to monitor them, as they all had an individual door facing the courtyard, either at ground level or from a balcony that afforded access to the first-floor rooms. Mike and a few of the senior "lieutenants" lived in the hotel, so they would be harder to track. Penny told us their room numbers and gave us a detailed description of the inside of the hotel.

I insisted, and Paul agreed, that I would be on the team that detained Rick. Not being a "fighting man" he would probably be one of the easier ones to subdue.

I was looking forward to it.

As the night wore on, we watched the raucous drink-fuelled "party" in silent fury.

Captain Digby summed it up: "This is one mission I haven't had to sell to the men. Given the chance, most of them would be down there now and taking them on hand-to-hand. They reckon they can make them suffer more that way, rather than sneaking up on them like thieves in the night."

As he left to talk to his men, he slapped me on the back and chuckled.

"Most of my men haven't been in the company of a woman for a long time and they're all feeling very chivalrous. But afterwards I might have to start putting bromide in their tea to help redirect their attention."

It was getting late now, and we watched the courtyard, as the men slowly drifted away, dragging their "prizes" with them. Some women appeared a short while later and accompanied a different man to another room. Paul paid close attention, all the while updating his plan, and marking which rooms were occupied.

It was after one o'clock by the time Mike, to a roar of approval from the few drunken men still remaining, swung his fist at Mel and struck her hard in the face. She stood reeling from the blow, and he picked her up, slung her over his shoulder and strode off like a conquering hero.

Paul spoke softly, "He's mine. No one else is to touch him."

With no women left to replenish the drinks and provide the entertainment, most of the human detritus that remained, staggered off to their respective rooms. Just a few were left to finish their bottles, and these soon drifted off to sleep.

The dying fire, aided by a bright moon and a clear night, gave us a good view of the area. For an hour, everything was quiet and then our attention was caught by movement at the front of the hotel.

It was Mel. And she was carrying a heavy load.

"What a star," Harry murmured, "she's gathered up a load of their shotguns, by the look of it."

We watched tensely as she glanced back at the building, gently lowered the guns to the ground and then proceeded to break them all down, hiding them against the side of the building behind some bushes. Turning in our direction, she tried some exaggerated but easily understood sign language.

Paul translated: "All asleep. Four in hotel. Nineteen in courtyard."

She crept across the courtyard and knocked quietly on one of the doors. Seconds later, Louise opened it and tiptoed out. She was holding another gun which she passed to Mel who, more practised by now, quickly broke it down and put it to one side.

"I'm sorry, guys, but she is amazing," said Paul admiringly. "She's doing all the hard work for us; all we're going to have to do is go down there and wake 'em up."

Harry and I glanced at each other in amusement, both struggling not to comment.

Paul interpreted our silence anyway, and glared at us both.

"Don't even go there, guys!" he said indignantly, at which point Harry snorted.

We recovered ourselves and turned our attention back to Mel and Louise, who were entering more rooms, and emerging from most of them with weapons, but occasionally accompanied by another of the women, wearing nothing more than a blanket and a confused look on her face.

Every time, Mel led the woman away from the building and was clearly telling them what was going to happen. You could follow the conversation by following where she was looking. Always at some point, their heads would turn and they would look towards the woods as she explained the plan. The looks of silent relief and joy on their faces was heartening to see. We watched Mel point and push one of the women gently towards a suitable hiding place. The woman crept obediently away into the darkness and crouched down behind a wall.

Mel was giving similar instructions to a second woman when…

"Shit!" Paul whispered urgently, "One of the guys by the fire is awake."

We watched with bated breath, as the man hauled himself up and struggled to collect his drunken, confused senses.

He made his way unsteadily towards the glowing embers of the fire and urinated. Scratching his backside and looking round at the men still asleep behind him, he staggered off towards one of the rooms.

Mel and her companion had spotted him, and were trying to conceal themselves in the shadows, staying as still as possible. The looks of frozen fear on their faces were plain to see through our high-powered binoculars.

The man spotted them and stopped abruptly, swaying on his feet as he prepared to call out to them.

We all half rose, preparing to grab what we needed and execute the plan early. If it was about to go wrong, we needed to improvise.

I threw the binoculars down, getting ready to go.

"Wait!" hissed Harry, and we all froze. He still had his binoculars trained on the target.

Paul and I grabbed ours and did the same.

Mel and the other woman had approached the man and had their arms draped over him.

In his befuddled state, he clearly wasn't able to deduce that this wasn't normal behaviour. A stupid smile appeared on his face and the two women led him towards an empty room. I thought about the way she'd handled Paul and I almost felt sorry for the man.

As the door closed behind them, Paul angrily but softly called for everyone to stand down.

"We go as planned!"

CHAPTER TWENTY-SIX

0400 hours

We all stood ready to go. Everyone carried rifles and ammunition. The only extra items with us were lengths of rope and plastic cable ties to immobilise our enemy quickly and effectively.

Everyone had been allocated rooms and targets and in theory, the plan was so simple it ought to succeed. But we'd all seen straightforward plans go badly wrong before, so I for one, was nervous about going in.

The idea was for everyone to move quietly into position and then wait for a quick short blast on a whistle to coordinate the start of the attack.

Speed and maximum aggression would then be the key to success.

Paul, Harry and I, accompanied by two other soldiers, would be responsible for taking Rick, Lucy, Mike and two other adults, all of whom were based in the main part of the hotel.

As requested, I was to be responsible for detaining Rick and Lucy. The spare soldiers would be responsible for securing them all with the rope and cable ties.

The hotel had a large function room and once this was secured, the prisoners would be brought there and guarded until the whole place had been taken, and order was restored.

With the familiar feeling of adrenaline surging through my veins, we set off down the hill to get into position. As we crept through the hotel, I reflected that it might have been better if we had taken our shoes off. In the dead of night, our footsteps sounded unnaturally loud.

But just as I chose to ignore the loud beating of my heart, I pushed aside my worries. Using the light of the moon that was streaming through the windows, I found the door that led to the suite of rooms Rick and his family were using.

I waited for the signal.

Minutes passed like hours.

Not daring to look at my watch, I waited impatiently, ready to switch on my headtorch, burst into the room and exact revenge on the person who had hurt us all so badly all those months ago.

The shrill short whistle blast came, and even though I'd been expecting it, it made me jump.

I'd experimented with the door handle gently when I'd first got into position, so I knew the door was locked.

Aiming my best kick at the door, I hoped fervently that the lock was as flimsy as it looked.

As the door burst open with a crash, I could hear shouts and screams emanating from other rooms.

Running into the lounge area of the two-bedroom suite Rick had claimed for himself, I screamed, "Everybody stay still! No one move!"

Penny had given me a good description of the layout of the suite.

As I ran towards the master bedroom, the door began to open. Kicking it as hard as I could, I heard a high-pitched scream and the sound of someone falling backwards as the door rebounded off a body.

I recognised the slightly nasal tones as the person called out for Mike to come and help him.

I stepped round the door and into the room and my torch showed Rick, sprawled across the bed, with his hands over his face, trying desperately to stem the flow of blood from his nose. The door had clearly hit his face when I'd kicked it.

Shame, I thought sarcastically, and stepped forward.

Lucy was sitting up in bed, whimpering in fear. Realising that the light from my headtorch was effectively blinding them and they couldn't see who was attacking them, I shouted at them to get off the bed and lie face down on the floor. It took a few kicks to get Rick to obey; he seemed to be finding it difficult to understand what was going on.

Looking at the mess I'd made of his nose I wondered if he had concussion, and then decided I didn't care.

I heard another door open and one of their children stuck their head out. At a bellow from me the door slammed shut again and I heard them both shrieking in terror in their room.

I pushed the thought of them aside. We'd have to deal with them later. My main objective was sobbing with fear on the floor at my feet.

I watched in disgust as a pool of urine spread across the carpet. The Emperor had wet himself.

The soldier arrived and quickly tied their hands behind their backs.

Before getting them to stand, I quickly secured the door handles to the children's room, more to keep them safe in one location than to imprison them.

It's not easy to stand up when you're lying face down on the floor, but after some shouts, threats and a couple of kicks of encouragement from me, they both managed it.

As they stood in front of me, snivelling and cowering, I couldn't help myself. The rage that had been building in me all this time came boiling to the surface.

"This is for Ian, you bastard." I stepped forward and punched him as hard as I could. The satisfaction it gave me made up for the sensation of bones cracking in my hand.

The blow knocked him over backwards. As he lay dazed on the floor, he realised what I had said.

Through his bleeding mouth he mumbled, "Who are you? Why are you doing this?"

Part of me was tempted to prolong the process but I knew there wasn't any point. As far as I was concerned, he was already condemned for all his actions. It was about time he knew how much trouble he was in.

"It's Tom, your old neighbour."

I could see his brain ticking over, processing what I'd said and trying desperately to turn the situation to his advantage.

"Tom! Christ! Thank God you're here!" he whined. "We've been prisoners here for months. What were you saying about Ian? I mean, I'm sorry I stole the car obviously. It was a moment of madness. I panicked. Look, we'll straighten this all out. I guess there must be some misunderstanding. I'll come back with you and I'll make a full apology for everything and then we'll carry on as before."

I lost it again. Forgetting all about the pain in my hand, I punched him a second time.

"You absolute bastard!" I screamed, half in anger, half in pain this time. "Ian is dead! You ran him over. Don't even try to deny it; plenty of people saw you do it. And if you think I'm going to believe anything else you tell me, DON'T BOTHER!

We've been watching you for days. We know exactly what you've been up to. Mel and Louise told us everything yesterday. Young Penny is sheltering in our OP in the woods, so your tame gorilla Mike can't get hold of her.

The country's got a plan for dealing with low life scum like you, and let me tell you, you've done more than enough to ensure you'll receive the maximum penalty."

He stared at me, his mouth opening and closing, and then fell to his knees.

"Please don't! I can explain everything. It's not my fault! I can't go to prison, I just can't."

I laughed, which made him stop sobbing and look at me with a confused expression on his face.

"Prison? No Rick. We don't have prisons anymore. For scum like you the death penalty's been reintroduced."

He looked at me in shocked silence.

Lucy started to scream.

I backed out of the room as the stench of his voiding bowels filled the air.

CHAPTER TWENTY-SEVEN

I stood at a distance from them, bathing Rick and Lucy in the light of my headlamp. Their pathetic behaviour sickened me, so I stood silently, the glare from my headtorch keeping them blind and confused.

Shouts and screams echoed through the building and from outside. I strained my ears to try to work out what was going on.

From what I could make out, the shouts were all commands and the screams were pleas for help or to be set free. We seemed to have the situation under control, but I wouldn't know for sure until someone arrived to escort the prisoners to the function room.

I shouted to Harry and Paul to check on their status. Harry replied that he was fine and was on his way to the function room with his prisoner. Then he'd be back to help.

Paul responded to say that Mike was being a bit "difficult", and he would wait for backup before he moved him.

Harry and another soldier arrived to help me transfer Rick and Lucy. They were still immobilised by panic and it took the three of us to manhandle them down the stairs and deposit them on the floor of the function room.

After a quick count, they were all present apart from one. It had to be Mike.

Captain Digby was in the middle of the room, making sure there were enough guards and that they were sufficiently distributed to cover the twenty-two sorry excuses for human beings who were currently occupying the space. None of them was offering any resistance and most had lapsed into a sullen silence.

I walked over to him. "Captain Digby, I take it everything went as planned out there? Everything seems OK in here. Once we've got that big bugger Mike downstairs we'll have a full house."

He grinned. "Call me Diggers, all my friends do. Yes, it all went smoothly. The women did a fantastic job. They were all still drunk and didn't have a clue what was happening until we had them secured, and by then it was too late for them to do anything.

Some of the women were a bit difficult to handle initially. A lot of them were screaming and hysterical, but the two who were helping you soon calmed them all down."

"Yes, Mel and Louise," I replied, looking round. "Where are they by the way? I just want to make sure they're OK."

Diggers nodded towards the main doors of the hotel, which were wide open. "I think they're still outside."

I turned and walked into the entrance hall just as Paul and three other soldiers were dragging a bellowing Mike down the stairs. He was fighting them every step of the way.

"Stop!" shouted Paul panting. "This is no good. We'll have to hog tie him and carry him." This was greeted by groans of disgust from the soldiers.

Ignoring them Paul said, "Get him on the floor now."

Mike had his hands tied in front of him, but was being held by three hefty looking men while Paul held him from behind with his arm firmly around his neck. It would have been enough to secure a normal person.

He was standing on a half landing, fiercely resisting the attempts to get him to the floor. Without warning he hurled himself forward, straight down the final flight of stairs, taking his hapless guards with him. Instinctively, they all let go to try to save themselves.

He rolled to his feet and with an incredible show of strength, broke the rope tying his hands together. All this had taken place in a heartbeat. Massaging his wrists to get the feeling back, he took a good look round the room, trying to decide what to do next.

We all raised our weapons.

"Don't shoot!"

Paul screamed the command, then bounded down the stairs and positioned himself between Mike and the only way out.

"Lower your weapons, everyone," he said, his eyes never leaving Mike's face, "it's too crowded in here. No one else is getting hurt because of some low life piece of scum who thinks beating up women up makes him look hard. I've got news for you pal, real men don't rape women."

Mike reddened and shot him a look of cold, naked hatred.

"Yep – we've heard all about you, you sick bastard," said Paul, quietly and deliberately. "Taking a fancy to young girls; bit of a pervert, aren't you? Guess you're not man enough to have a proper relationship?"

Looking around I could see what Paul was doing. He'd caused enough of a delay for every available soldier to move into position. Mike was surrounded. There was no way he was going to be able to fight everyone, but he was still big enough to hurt a lot of people before they managed to subdue him.

Slowly, calmly, Paul took a step towards him.

"Tell you what mate, if you want to prove how much of a man you are, why don't you try and get past me? You're going to die today anyway, so why not try and take me with you?"

A loud muttering started up, and a few of the men shouted in support of Paul. Then the room fell quiet again, and it was as if everyone had simultaneously held their breath. Mike scowled and took a good look round, then seemed to come to a decision.

He knew his fate. He was surrounded by heavily armed men. He knew he wasn't going to be able to get away.

He let out a roar and ran at Paul, spreading his arms to try to grab him in a bear hug.

Paul was quicker. He waited till he was almost on him, then calmly ducked under his outstretched arms and tapped his ankle as he passed, tripping him up.

We all watched intently, drawn into this violent display of power and control.

Mike intended to kill Paul and Paul intended to make him suffer for what he had done.

As Mike fell heavily, we let out a roar of approval. Our man had outsmarted the enemy.

The room crackled with primeval excitement.

Mike let out a thundering roar and struggled to his feet. Twice more he ran at Paul and each time he was effortlessly tripped up. Each time, Paul goaded him into getting back up on his feet.

On his next and final charge, Mike attempted to anticipate Paul's sidestep, and jinked away at the last second, hoping to catch him out. Paul was ready for him. He stepped in and kicked him hard in the groin.

Mike crumpled to the ground, his high-pitched screams filling the room.

Paul shouted to be heard, "Gag him and tie him up properly this time."

We all cheered. Paul hadn't even broken a sweat and he had bested one of the biggest men I'd ever seen.

It was the kind of fight that would be talked about around the fire for years to come, with bragging rights for anyone who could say they were actually there.

The excitement over, Mike was carried out, his screams muffled by a rag stuffed into his mouth, and dumped in the function room along with all the other prisoners. Paul, after extricating himself from a throng of well-wishers, joined me and Harry and we walked outside. Someone had thrown more wood on to the fire and we could see that the women had been drawn to it like a beacon of hope.

They all seemed to be finding the sudden change in their fortunes hard to grasp. Mel and Louise were talking to them all and offering words of hope and encouragement.

Mel noticed us approach and walked straight up to Paul. Standing awkwardly before him she said, "Thank you. I saw what you did to Mike."

She took his watch off her wrist and handed it back to him. On the verge of tears, she turned and walked back to the other women.

Paul stood and stared at her.

Harry and I exchanged smiles. To break the silence, Harry chipped in, "Better go and get Great Grandpapa's watch back I suppose," and strolled off, whistling.

The women were understandably all very emotional, but there was joy too. There wasn't much we could do apart from offer them some words of comfort and support, but as they seemed much more impressed by what Harry had to say, I gave in and stood to one side. A few minutes later, I felt a tug at my sleeve.

It was Penny.

"I know you told me to stay in the woods," she said anxiously, "but I could see everything was OK so I came down. I hope you don't mind?"

I smiled at her, "Not at all, young lady. It's perfectly safe here now, so you've done the right thing,"

She flushed with pleasure at my approval.

The first light of dawn was appearing on the eastern horizon. It was going to be a sunny day by the look of it.

Regardless of the weather, we had some serious business to take care of today.

It was time to convene a court and put the prisoners on trial for their lives.

CHAPTER TWENTY-EIGHT

Now that the prisoners were properly secured and under guard, the mood relaxed.

The hotel kitchens were still in reasonable working order, thanks to a large propane tank in the grounds. In no time at all, a few of the soldiers had been detailed to kitchen duty. Soon mugs of tea were being handed out and unidentifiable food, concocted from whatever was available, was being cooked in large frying pans and distributed.

We were all so ravenous it tasted delicious anyway.

Harry had intervened and ordered the women out of the kitchen. They'd lived in horrendous conditions for months and been worked like slaves. Now it was their turn to sit down and be waited on. This simple act of kindness on Harry's part led to a few of them breaking down in tears again, but they soon recovered enough to enjoy what was given to them.

Although everyone was exhausted after a night without sleep, the general mood was buoyant.

Radio calls had been made, passing on the news that the mission had been a success. Harry had even read out a short message of congratulation from the Queen; a novel experience for everyone.

For logistical reasons, the decision was taken to accommodate everyone overnight in the hotel.

A lot of details had to be agreed upon and arrangements needed to be made. There was very little of value at the hotel apart from an insignificant amount of food, which we quickly catalogued and sorted. The only weapons to speak of were shotguns, apart from a World War Two service revolver which had been found in Rick's bedroom.

It was agreed that the shotguns and ammunition should be split between the two groups. Half would be kept by our community to add to our stores and half would be returned to the base for distribution as they saw fit.

The revolver mysteriously disappeared into someone's rucksack.

I don't know why, I just liked it.

As midday approached, the trial started.

The trial procedures we had developed had moved on over time, but one basic principle was still adhered to.

The senior officer present resided as judge, while a selection of others present acted as the jury.

No notes were taken and the defendant had one chance to answer the accusations the judge put to him, prior to the sentence being decided by a jury vote. A simple majority vote decided whether the defendant was innocent or guilty.

Life or death. A simple but tough choice.

If witnesses were available, they were given the opportunity to confirm or deny the accusations against the accused. If someone wished to defend the accused, they were given one chance to sway the jury.

It wasn't a kangaroo court; it was simply the only workable solution we had been able to come up with in order to reach the right decision with limited resources.

Harry would reside as the judge and the jury would consist of twelve randomly selected soldiers.

I volunteered, along with all the women, to be called as witnesses.

One by one, the men who had followed Rick and caused so much suffering, were called forward to face the charges against them.

For most of them it was an easy decision for the jury to make.

The tearful testimony of one of the women, as she described the acts committed by the individual against her, was enough to condemn the man to death.

Pleas for clemency were granted only twice, when a woman spoke up to defend the individuals in question, describing some act of kindness that had saved her or someone else from unnecessary suffering.

Mike's trial was the quickest of all.

Finally, the only people remaining to be dealt with were Rick and Lucy.

They both had to be dragged to stand trial and they refused to cooperate in any way. After the charges were read, I stood and gave an account of how he had killed Ian after stealing our community's Land Rover all those months ago.

Further testimonies were given by quite a few of the women, Mel and Louise included, and these painted a grim picture of cruelty, domination and a selfish disregard for anyone except themselves.

When they were offered the chance to defend their actions, all they did was cry and plead for forgiveness. They offered no justifications for their actions. Finally, Harry ended the matter by declaring them guilty and they were given the death sentence.

The usual form of execution was by firing squad, but Harry gave the order for Rick, Lucy and Mike to be hanged for their crimes. No other sentence, he declared, could recompense for their vile and selfish actions.

The three of them were dragged away to await their fates.

As was the tradition, we all drew lots for firing squad duty.

I was one of the men elected.

This would be a first for me and I expected to be more nervous and apprehensive about it. Yes, I'd killed people in self-defence, but this would be the first time I had been asked to take the life of someone who was not an immediate threat to me or the people around me.

But I felt no sympathy for any of them. They had to die for what they had done. The liberal world of forgiveness and compassion had disappeared without trace, and been replaced by one in which every wrong action had to be punished.

The condemned men were lined up, five at time, facing ten of us.

Once I'd carried out my duty, I walked away and spent half an hour on my own. I noticed some of the others did the same.

Guilty or not guilty, it would have been wrong to feel nothing about taking their lives. That, I reasoned, was what set me apart from people like them.

As a suitable gallows had yet to be built, Rick, Lucy and Mike's sentences would be carried out the following morning. It would also give the couple time to say goodbye to their children.

While we had no qualms about what was going to happen to their parents, Michael and Richard were a different matter. Their parents would die because of their actions, but essentially the children had done nothing wrong. And yet having your parents killed was about as big a punishment as you could get.

We couldn't think of a solution. All the women agreed that the children had displayed vindictive behaviour. They had abused their position and enjoyed having "servants" to tend to them.

They had made a game out of inventing misdemeanours and reporting them to Mike, who could always be relied upon to administer swift and harsh punishment on the person who had fallen foul of them.

I was sure a psychologist could have found all sorts of reasons and excuses for their behaviour, but as far as I was concerned, they had been precocious, horrible little individuals before and having a father with so much power had done nothing to temper their dispositions since.

We asked the question, but understandably, none of the women would consider taking them on. I couldn't blame them. They would be a constant reminder of a terrible period in their lives and they hadn't exactly endeared themselves to anyone. For the same reason, I didn't think it would be appropriate for them to return to the road with us.

Though not a satisfactory solution by any means, it was finally decided that they would be taken to the base and placed in the care of a foster family.

They would be monitored from time to time and hopefully they would grow up into the kind of men who would be an asset to the country, rather than another couple of bad apples who were likely to cause more trouble.

If they took the second path, that bridge would have to be crossed when we came to it.

In terms of the transport on site, the good news was that the six Land Rovers parked in the yard were all in good working order.

Our group was offered all of them, but we decided that three would be enough. We already had a few military vehicles permanently stationed at our compound and they were infrequently used. We told the people at the base to use them as they saw fit.

With Captain Digby and his men taking care of guard duty and sorting through and allocating any useful supplies and equipment from the hotel, we found ourselves with the luxury of a few hours off.

After returning and dismantling our OP in the woods, we took the time to talk to and get to know the women we had helped to rescue.

Although they were all still coming to terms with their sudden release, they were obviously elated at their good fortune.

We asked them where they would like to go and answered all their questions about the base and our compound to the best of our abilities.

I explained that there were regular trips between the two locations and therefore if it didn't work out for them at one place, they could easily move to the other. About half of them said they would like to try life at our compound first, as they liked our description of the small friendly community we had created. The rest preferred the idea of being part of a far larger and better defended community.

So far, Mel had not indicated where she wanted to go, and watching from the sidelines, I noticed that she was constantly looking at Paul when she thought no one was looking.

Paul, for his part, had made several attempts to engage her in conversation, but so far, he'd had little success.

As he was blind to the obvious, I took him by the elbow and led him away so that we could have a private chat.

Following my success with Allan and Michelle (well OK, that was partly down to Becky) I considered myself an expert on relationships. I'd said as much to Becky and to my annoyance she'd laughed so hard she couldn't stand for five minutes.

Women, I concluded, lacked the depth of understanding we men have at times.

"Paul!" I said brightly, "what's up? Oh no, let me guess. Mel's avoiding you like the plague and you don't know why?"

Looking slightly uncomfortable, he said, "Yes. I know what she's been through and I don't want to upset her, but I would like to get to know her better. She just won't look at me."

"Trust me," I said, "she is! Every time you aren't looking at her, she's watching you. Try this for a theory: she's had a bloody terrible time of it. You turn up – her knight in shining armour - sickeningly muscle bound and handsome,"

I added, just to make him squirm a bit. "She likes you, but knows that you know what she's been through. She probably, and very wrongly, I might add, feels ashamed and not very good about herself because of it."

I clapped him on his shoulder. "Now, my young apprentice, why don't you march in there, and tell her it would be great if she chose to come and stay with us because you'd really love to get to know her better? Tell her you understand that she'll need some time but you think she's the most incredibly brave and beautiful woman you've ever met. That should do for starters!"

He looked at me and his handsome face lit up. He turned and walked back towards the crowd, craning his neck to look for Mel.

"Don't thank me, it's what I do!" I called to his retreating back.

A few minutes later I could see a tearful but smiling Mel and a beaming Paul chatting away.

I couldn't wait to tell Becky about my latest triumph, I thought smugly.

CHAPTER TWENTY-NINE

I took a last glance through my rear-view mirror at the three bodies, slowly swinging from the gallows, as I drove down the driveway away from the hotel and turned towards home.

Harry, Paul and I had taken a vehicle each, leaving plenty of room for the six women, including Mel, Louise and Penny, who had chosen to return with us. The vehicles also contained the few personal possessions the women owned and all the supplies we had gathered from the hotel, which amounted to a very small amount of food, but a very large quantity of alcohol. On top of all that we had stacked various useful items we had scavenged from the hotel.

We'd only been away a few days, but we were all eager to get home and see our families and friends.

We knew that everyone would be busy preparing for the new arrivals and that they would receive the warmest welcome possible.

As I drove along, chatting to Louise and Penny, who had both chosen to travel with me, my mind wandered.

People attribute a lot of things that happen to Fate.

Other people call it coincidence, but Fate must be real.

How else could I be driving the very same car I had first sat in and started all those months ago, when I was helping Jerry and his family move.

I'd met Jerry before Day One of the event at a random encounter in the local cash and carry; was that Fate or coincidence?

The one thing that had been missing from our fledgling community had been medical expertise, and I'd managed to bump into and make friends with a doctor whose wife was a dentist. Fate?

The commander of the base was Jerry's brother.

Our community had only survived because of the timely arrival of Colonel Jon Moore and his forces, who had not only helped us to defeat Gumin and his men, but had also wiped out the escaped prisoners, who would certainly have found us and annihilated us with their superior weapons and military training.

It was almost as if Fate needed good to prevail over evil and had therefore set in motion a chain of events that had led me to be sitting in a familiar vehicle, making my way back to my family after another successful mission.

All of this from a chance meeting at a cash and carry in Stirchley, Birmingham.

Fate?

Mind boggling really.

I dragged myself back to the present, and concentrated on the road and the conversation going on in the car.

After a few nights of interrupted rest and a full night of no sleep, I was glad I'd spent the previous night in a comfortable hotel bed. I knew that the arrival of new residents in our community would lead to a big celebration. Opportunities for a celebration didn't come around very often, so we made the most of them when they did.

It was our way of compensating for all the hard work we had to put in to make the community thrive.

Festivals and public holidays in every corner of the globe must have developed for the same reason. People need to be able to let off steam occasionally and a good old party was one way of doing just that. I grinned to myself. The fact that I would be unloading a large amount of booze would help.

Hours later, long after we'd arrived home, I snuggled thankfully up to Becky in bed.

The new arrivals soon settled into the community. Over the first few days and weeks, they spent a lot of time with Michelle, Kim and Mandy who had all had similar experiences in the past.

Everyone else carried on as before, our time continually split between security work and community projects. We remained on high alert. To let your guard down for just one minute, could invite disaster. The only thing that would guarantee our safety would be our own vigilance.

The scavenging missions had all but ceased, as we had finally stripped out everything useful from the areas around us. Our scavenging missions had been replaced by long-range patrol and reconnaissance missions, lasting many days, systematically exploring an ever-widening radius around us.

They either bivouacked somewhere suitable or stayed with one of the friendly communities we had links with.

These patrols inevitably led to the discovery of more groups and individuals who had managed to survive.

Unfortunately, they also revealed the extent of the devastation caused by the plague. There were whole communities reduced to a scattering of rotting corpses. The really sad part was, there was clear evidence that some of them had been doing well. Like us, they'd had defences, weapons and storerooms full of food.

None of these things had been any use against the plague. Without the benefit of any advanced warning, they'd stood little chance.

As before, most of the people they encountered proved friendly, despite their initial reservations, once they realised that our intentions were good. Again, many of them signed up for government assistance and in return, agreed to contribute towards the country's recovery.

If they were disinclined to be welcoming, then that was OK too. We left them to it, making a note of their location for future reference. If they'd been tough enough to survive for so long without help and didn't want or need our assistance, then we had to respect that.

If they were overtly aggressive and attacked us without provocation, then plans were put in place to deal with them, as they would always be a threat to the brave new world we were trying to create.

More often than not, we were alerted to the presence of these groups by other communities in their locality, who had had been threatened or attacked by them.

Call us vigilantes, militia or a police force, we had the full backing and approval of the government and we knew that there was no room for that kind of hostility in the society we were working towards.

Back at the compound, the one thing that took up most of our time was Pete's latest idea.

He called it Project Grow!

With the help of some experts at the base, he had managed to work out how much land we needed to cultivate and what variety of crops would work best, in order to feed us all and enable us to become fully self-sufficient.

His findings had shown that we didn't have anywhere near enough land prepared. We considered clearing more back gardens, but we knew that this would be a huge task and would necessitate the removal of trees, paths etc.

The solution, once we'd thought of it, was obvious.

We'd looked before at the many allotments in the area and discounted them due to concerns about irrigation if we happened to have a long dry summer. Supplemental water couldn't be drawn from a tap anymore.

Cannon Hill Park had proved to be the ideal location. A former recreational park, it was a huge open area covering hundreds of acres and was less than a mile away. It had large lakes that had been used for boating and the River Rea flowed alongside it. These sources would provide more than enough water for irrigation.

We just needed Russ to work his magic again.

Every available hand was called in to prepare the ground for planting and erect acres of polytunnels.

He was confident, with the work we had already done, which would soon be yielding fresh produce, that within a year we would be completely self-sufficient. In fact, we might even be producing a surplus.

The possibility of producing a surplus was something that had generated a lot of debate. Should we try to store it in case of future problems (e.g. crop failure or bad weather)? Or should we donate it to people who needed it? Or, as someone later suggested, could we trade it for something we needed?

The third suggestion opened up a further discussion about the future. Once the country had stabilised and people had settled down to the business of living, and given up trying to kill and steal from each other, then hopefully communities like ours would proliferate.

Possibly, depending on their locations, these other communities might all have something to offer and at this point we could foresee trade developing between them.

The amateur historians among us pointed out that this could also lead to wars being fought for control over the most productive areas.

Subjects like these became our favourite topics for discussion once the darkness was setting in and we'd stopped work to gather together in the communal kitchen.

Of course, our arguments were all purely theoretical. We were still a long way from becoming self-sufficient, but at the same time, this was a turning point for our community.

For the first time, we weren't just thinking about surviving day-to-day, as we had been just after the event. And we weren't just looking to the immediate future, as we had done when we had sufficient supplies to last us for a few months. Now we were beginning to think about the years ahead.

This new confidence of ours would stand us in good stead.

CHAPTER THIRTY

Summer had finally arrived and the community was thriving. After a long convalescence, Allan was back to full health and had resumed his role as security officer.

Having undergone a series of operations to repair the damage to his face, Gary had returned with his wife and daughter and settled back into his life among us. Despite his scars and the loss of his eye, he was happy to be home and said he felt grateful to be alive.

Harry had become a permanent resident on the road, and he and Kim were very much in love. They had moved in together and willingly taken on Isaac and Lottie, and were now a very close and loving family unit.

Harry had even taken Kim back to the base to meet the Queen, Prince Philip and his brother and sister-in-law (William and Kate).

She came back beaming and was immediately swept away by the women for a full debrief.

Harry watched them go and picked up a can of beer. He took a swig, looked at us, winked and said,

"Sorted!"

Michelle and Allan's relationship was also flourishing, and despite frequent enquiries from all of us, they refused to confirm whether they had set a date for their wedding yet.

We suspected that something was afoot, but no matter how hard we tried to wheedle it out of them, they remained tight-lipped on the matter.

My main worry, which was an indication of how well we were doing, was how long my precious hoard of chocolate hobnobs was going to last me. During the madness of stocking up with as much food as we could buy, prior to the event, I had bought every single packet I could lay my hands on. With careful rationing, I'd managed to eke them out for as long as possible, but now I was down to my last few packs.

My anxiety had been a source of great amusement for everyone else and it was a standing joke now that whenever a patrol was about to leave, someone would shout, "Don't forget the hobnobs!" I'd heard so many false reports about sightings of them, I'd stopped believing any of them.

We hardly ever saw anyone at our barricades now. The only people who did drift by from time to time were those who had chosen a nomadic existence, roving through abandoned and empty cities, towns and villages and gathering up whatever they could find as they went.

Modern day gypsies, I suppose you could call them.

Good manners dictated that we should offer these people a meal, but we were more than happy to do so. These people had survived without walls around them.

They carried weapons for protection and they lived on their wits. That meant that on their travels they picked up all sorts of useful information.

Information we could use.

Some of them had even made a living out of it, carrying messages between the communities, and passing on information in return for a meal or two.

The intricate networks of society were starting to repair themselves.

In the meantime, the news from the base was all positive. The plans to rebuild were in full swing and groups were beginning to spread out from the base to start farming and developing their own communities.

Undoubtedly, mistakes would be made and things would go wrong from time to time, but as everyone was working towards a single goal, eventually they would succeed.

Attacks on these newly formed communities were rare. The composition of each group was carefully thought out to include a broad mix of people, all with different skills. This included a few soldiers plus equipment and weapons. Careful planning also went into the locations of these new communities.

They were far enough away from each other to allow room for expansion, but close enough to maintain contact and offer each other assistance if required. For instance, extra manpower might be needed at harvest time, or for security purposes.

After losing so many of us to the plague, our compound seemed a little empty. The familiar faces of people we had shared so much with, would never be seen again.

Some of the more artistic members of our community had turned an outside wall of the church into a memorial for the people we had lost. The names of all our absent friends had been lovingly painted on to it. Friends and family members had followed suit by adding pictures and mementos. It had become a place of quiet contemplation and healing; somewhere to remember old friends and happy memories. And somewhere to shed a tear.

In rare quiet moments, I found myself drawn to the wall.

Not a day went by when I didn't feel blessed that my own family had survived, and the wall was a constant reminder of how fragile life is.

The plague had had other consequences for our community. We'd lost more women than men to the disease and this had resulted in the men outnumbering the women by some margin. In fact, it soon became clear that the disparity between the sexes would have to be addressed before it became a problem.

The young single males in our group were mostly soldiers who had volunteered to remain with us. They had become important and useful members of our community, not least because they were all young and fit and were able to take on most of the heavy work.

But being young and male, it was amazing how often they would appear when the young single females were out doing their chores, offering their assistance with whatever task they were performing.

It was all very chivalrous and good natured, as everyone knew what the women had been through, but as time wore on it became clear that this good-natured competition for love would eventually lead to friction in the group.

Much to the embarrassment of certain younger members of the group, who believed their behaviour had been discreet, the topic was brought up for discussion at an evening meeting.

Allan made a valid point:

"It's not just the youngsters we need to think about. The plague has left behind single parents too. I know it's too soon for any of them to be thinking about it, but in the future, when their wounds are healed and they're ready to accept someone else into their lives, in a community as small as ours, potential partners are going to be hard to come by.

If we're going to prosper, I think we'll need to think about expanding our population. But, if we do, we'll need to give careful thought to who we invite to join us."

Over the next few months the community did expand. We didn't just invite the strong and physically fit.

After careful consultations with the base, a wide variety of people helped to make our community whole again. Be they young or old, male or female, they all came with the kind of skills we needed and the type of personality that would fit in with us all.

As relationships were formed, Pete joked about asking the base for a supply of bromide, so that he could start adding it to the morning tea to calm all the raging hormones.

Allan and Michelle finally announced their wedding date. It was going to take place on the summer solstice, the longest day and shortest night of the year in the northern hemisphere. We had always planned to celebrate the summer and winter solstices, as in years gone by, but now the summer solstice was going to be a big party.

It would be the first marriage to take place in the UK since the event.

CHAPTER THIRTY-ONE

As the day approached, the preparations intensified.

The event was to receive the full backing of the base. The following message came back from Colonel Moore:

"Her Majesty the Queen offers the full support of the government to help celebrate this momentous event. Any assistance or equipment will, if at all possible, be made available."

A civil ceremony was planned and the registrar was expected to arrive the day before the wedding on a convoy of invited guests from the base.

Engineers had arrived in lorries loaded with equipment, and were busy erecting a small tented village to provide temporary accommodation for all the visitors.

Michelle was too wrapped up in her own preparations to notice all the extra activity taking place, but Allan was not taking it well, particularly as he had overheard a radio conversation between Paul and the base about the extra security that would be required for the Prime Minister and the other VIPs.

The quiet, simple wedding he'd envisioned, celebrated with a few good friends, was now a beast running out of control and he didn't like it one bit.

He complained loudly to Pete, Harry, Paul and myself, but had the sense to keep his feelings from Michelle. He didn't want anything to ruin her day, and as she was oblivious to what was happening, he was determined to keep it that way. He told her that the extra accommodation was for the people they had befriended from nearby communities, who had insisted on coming to celebrate their special day with them.

It was partly the truth, as some of the accommodation was for them.

His stag night, held at Michelle's insistence, a few days before the event, took place in the tennis pavilion of Chantry Tennis Club, in the park our road backed on to.

The tennis courts had long since been turned over to polytunnels, and the historic wooden clubhouse, a place that held happy memories for most of the road's original residents, had been left intact. No one had had the heart to knock it down so now it stood there forlornly, looking increasingly more exposed, as the trees around it were cut down one by one for firewood.

Michelle's hen night was held on the same night in the church hall. Harry had managed to arrange for disco equipment to be delivered and set up in the hall as a surprise. I never found out how. So, the women got to spend the night dancing (probably to cheesy music) while the men settled for darts, pool, beer and banter.

I'm not sure who had the wildest night, but Harry's account of barely escaping with his life, following a quick visit to the girls to check that everything was working OK, had us all in stitches.

As Allan had done me the great honour of asking me to be his best man, I took my duties seriously and ensured that his memory of most of the night was hazy but happy.

Formalities were observed, and Michelle and Allan spent the night before the wedding apart.

As he was unable to sleep because of nerves, I spent most of the night sitting with him in our favourite planning spot, the hut on the main barricade, drinking coffee and chatting. As the sun rose at about 5.30 in the morning, we gave up on the possibility of sleep, and carrying a weapon each, spent the next few hours walking the perimeter until it was time for us to get ready.

I had been looking after Allan's police ceremonial uniform, which had been delivered from the base.

Michelle was expecting to see him in a standard suit, so seeing him resplendent in his uniform was going to be just one of the surprises planned for the day.

A large marquee had been erected for the ceremony, on the main road in Moseley village. At the allotted hour, we all began to gather. Becky was with Michelle, so I tried in vain to keep Stanley and Daisy from running around with their friends and ruining their immaculate clothes. Other parents were attempting to do the same, with varying degrees of success.

Everyone had made an effort and dressed in their finest clothes. Most of us were delighted at the opportunity to get dressed up, something we all thought we wouldn't be doing again.

The soldiers looked fantastic in their dress uniforms. As a member of the royal household, Harry's was particularly impressive. Kim was breathtakingly pretty in a dress she'd found from somewhere.

Paul Berry stood proudly next to Mel. After a very gentle courtship, they were now very much in love and had continued to look after Penny whom they loved like a daughter.

Everyone was smiling and enjoying the occasion. Chris Garland stood laughing with Pete and the others. He had met a woman recently, while running a survival course at another community. He had invited her along to the wedding and we all had hopes that the relationship would develop.

Well known political figures, including the prime minister and his family, were milling around and exchanging pleasantries with everyone, and enjoying the sunshine. The wide gulf that had previously existed between high profile politicians and personalities, and the general public, had long since disappeared.

I spotted Harry walking over to Allan with a serious expression on his face. I knew what it was about, so I quickly put on my game face.

"We have a problem. The registrar has fallen ill. I've just been to check on her, and there's no way she's going to be able to perform the ceremony," he said frowning.

Allan went slightly pale, pulled out a handkerchief and wiped his forehead.

"Can we delay it?" he stammered, "what am I going to tell Michelle? I knew it was all going too well …"

He stopped when he noticed that Harry was trying, and failing, to suppress a smile.

"What's so funny?" Allan snapped.

"Oh, nothing dear chap," Harry replied, trying and failing to look serious.

Allan glared at him.

"I know you, posh boy! You only act like that when you're up to something. Tell me! I'm on edge enough as it is. Today is not the day to wind me up."

Harry checked his watch and cocked his ear, as if listening for something.

"Allan, my good friend. Trust me, there is no way I'd really wind you up on a day like today. It's just that some surprises are just that. Surprises."

I could now hear the faint whump of a helicopter approaching.

The noise gradually grew louder, until two helicopters appeared overhead and circled the compound slowly.

"What's going on? Who's coming now?" Allan shouted above the increasing din, as they slowly began to settle and prepare for landing.

I was smiling now too, as I'd been let in on the secret only a few hours before. Harry hadn't wanted the downwash from the helicopter to ruin Michelle's carefully coiffured hair, so he'd told us both what he had planned and asked Becky to keep Michelle inside until after the helicopters' arrival.

A curious crowd gathered around the two helicopters, as their rotor blades slowly stopped spinning. The side door on the first helicopter opened and a soldier ran forward and placed some steps up to the door.

Her Majesty Queen Elizabeth II appeared in the doorway and took Harry's proffered hand for support, as she stepped from the helicopter followed by Prince Phillip.

The crowd broke into spontaneous applause, which increased in volume as the Duke and Duchess of Cambridge stepped from the other helicopter.

Allan turned to me and saw the smile on my face.

"You knew?"

I nodded.

"Only for a few hours, my friend. Harry told us what was happening this morning."

He frowned.

"But there can't be a wedding. We don't have a registrar."

I laughed.

"There never was a registrar. The person you met yesterday was an aide to one of the ministers pretending she knew what she was talking about."

"Well how the hell are we going to get marr…"

A look of panic came over his face, as it occurred to him that the Head of the Church of England, the Defender of the Faith, had just stepped from the helicopter. I watched as his brain kept suggesting and then dismissing the possibility that the Queen might be performing the marriage ceremony.

I slapped him on the back.

"Yes, mate, she is! Harry put the idea to her a few weeks ago, and she agreed that it was an unusual but wonderful proposal. No one could confirm if she could legally perform the ceremony, so I believe she used her royal prerogative to decree that she can."

He was lost for words. He looked at me and his eyes filled with tears.

"I can't believe it. I just wanted a quiet wedding to confirm my love for the woman I want to spend the rest of my life with. There I was moaning about what a circus it was becoming, but I take it all back. Michelle's going to get the wedding of her dreams. I can't thank you all enough!"

A look of trepidation settled on his face, as he saw Harry leading the Queen directly towards him.

I whispered theatrically, "Keep calm and remember your manners."

He had no time to respond, but my remark seemed to have the desired effect because he began to look calmer.

Harry made the formal introductions.

The ceremony, which was delayed for a few hours due to the Queen's arrival and the need to make a few changes in the marquee, couldn't have gone better.

Michelle looked truly beautiful in her dress, and radiated happiness. The look on her face when she saw Allan in his uniform was everything we had hoped for.

The Queen, looking magnificent in a fur gown and the crown jewels, performed the ceremony with great dignity, and there wasn't a dry eye in sight.

The day meant so much to us all. It wasn't just a celebration of a wedding; it was setting the scene for the future.

After the wedding breakfast the Queen gave a rousing speech thanking everyone present for the contribution they had made to the recovery of the UK. It was through all our efforts, she stressed, that the country had not only picked itself up after the event, but was beginning to prosper again. Her speech concluded, she set off back to the base.

Much later, I sat with a drink in my hand, grateful for the opportunity to have a few moments to myself. The evening was warm and balmy and seemed to last for ever.

I looked round the marquee at all the people who were important to me: my family and my friends, particularly my former neighbours. We had all put so much work into the community we had created and into this place we called home.

Not really knowing why, I walked out of the marquee and down the road.

The security cordon provided by the base for our protection had been widened to include the temporary accommodation, so the gates to the compound were sitting open and unmanned.

I found myself sitting in my usual lookout post on the wall. I found its familiarity comforting. As I sat enjoying the peace, my mind began to wander. We had achieved so much already, what would the future hold?

I leaned back and closed my eyes.

Ten Years in the Future

I sat watching the traditional summer solstice celebrations.

Allan came up and handed me a bottle of homemade wine.

"We're getting better at this wine making. This year's vintage is the best yet; remember our early efforts? It tasted like paint stripper, but it was all we had."

I grimaced and made choking sounds at the memory.

We were interrupted by Allan's son, Billy running up and jumping on to his lap. He was eight and full of energy.

After a couple of minutes of tickling and hugging, he ran off to rejoin his friends, who were making the most of being allowed to stay up late.

He called after him, "Don't forget to include your sister. She may be younger than you but she loves playing with you."

Billy turned and shouted, "No, Dad! Katie's OK, look she's over there playing with her friends."

Before Allan could respond, he was out of sight.

I topped both our glasses up and we clinked them together.

"Happy anniversary, mate," I said.

"I know. Ten years! Who would have thought it? And where has the time gone?"

"Some would say it's been non-stop hard work. But not me!" I replied, grinning.

I twisted in my seat to look around.

The many windows of the large country house we now lived in were brightly lit with lamps and candles.

In the fading light, I could still see the acres of crops and fields full of livestock we tended and nurtured to feed our community.

"Well, at least we know now that it was the right decision to leave the city. It was crumbling around us. We're much better off out here. This one building, although it might be old and cold in the winter, is so much easier to maintain than all the houses we used to live in. The fields are easier to tend and the surrounding properties still give us room to expand."

He nudged me in the ribs and my eyes were drawn to Stan, who stood there laughing with his arm around his partner, Grace. Grace was heavily pregnant.

"Yes, yes thanks for reminding me I'm going to be a grandad," I murmured with a smile on my face.

Stan had grown into a man to be proud of. Handsome and strong, he was also a valuable member of the community. He'd met Grace during a visit to a neighbouring community.

After a long-distance courtship, he'd eventually persuaded her to come and live with him.

And as marriages had created alliances between kingdoms in the past, so the joining of two young members from separate communities created bonds that strengthened the relationships between them.

"What time are you off in the morning, Tom?"

"Oh, not too early," I replied, raising my glass. "It'll take two days to get to the base on horseback. I'm going to pick up some of the other council members on the way so that we can travel together."

A few years before, I had been asked to join a new initiative. The old politicians and leaders of the past had conceded that their skills and experience were no longer relevant in the world we occupied now.

Instead it was agreed that each area of communities would be represented by one council member, and these council members would come together periodically to discuss any matters raised.

Some of the issues could be agreed over the radio, but it was always best to meet face to face to get the more serious matters agreed.

Although all the communities could stay in contact with each other via radio, the crumbling roads had made travel by anything but horseback an arduous task and therefore visiting anybody but your nearest neighbour was difficult. For this reason, all the members for the entire country would get together at one large meeting and these were held every six months or so.

The dates varied depending on the time of year, and the workloads of the communities, but as it took most of the council members several days to reach the base in Herefordshire (which was still the country's "seat of power"), the meetings usually lasted at least a couple of days so that all the matters could be covered in that time.

I had been persuaded to accept the role.

"It's going to be a good get together," I remarked, "the trade routes are working really well now. And there'll be enough surplus this year to enable more coal mines to open.

They're also hoping to get more steam trains running soon, which will make it much easier to move the supplies around the country to where they're needed."

Alan laughed.

"It's great, isn't it? If I had told anyone before this happened that steam trains and horse-drawn canal barges were going to be the only economical and feasible way to deliver goods around the country, I'd have been locked up."

"Yes, but the good thing is, apart from critical goods such as coal and salt, not much else needs to be delivered. We've all learned to live on what we can produce locally," I pointed out.

"So, that bottle of brandy we shared the other day was what?" he said, filling up my wine glass again, and smiling.

"That was a gesture of goodwill from our friends across the Channel. The sailing boats that regularly cross the Channel don't just carry people. Trade between countries is important," I replied, trying to look important and indignant at the same time.

"That bottle was sent to me personally by the President of France. She sent a gift to each council member. You should feel honoured I've even shared it with you!"

"I dare you to send her a bottle of our home-made plonk to show her the best the UK has to offer."

I laughed, almost spitting out a mouthful of wine.

"No way! Wars have been started for less. No, seriously though, the main agenda items are about trying to work out how big our food surplus will be this year.

That way, we can work out how many extra people we can feed and allocate to all the others jobs that need doing. I've mentioned coal mining and salt production, but we plan to expand the regional hospital programme too.

Those buildings need to be staffed and maintained, and the roads leading to them need to be kept in good repair.

When I took the job as council member on, I didn't realise the half of it. Everything we improve creates more problems that then need to be looked at."

Alan slapped me on the back.

"Rather you than me. I'm happy here with Michelle and the children. Security hasn't been an issue for years and I can't remember the last time I was called out to resolve anything more than bickering neighbours who just needed their heads knocking together to see sense. The first couple of years were a bit more interesting until those few rotten apples were removed from the barrel."

Alan had been made Chief of Regional Police, a job he had done single-handedly, looking after security and policing matters for our own and other neighbouring communities.

As most communities had their own internal policing policies, it was rarely necessary for Allan to intervene. And we all still possessed weapons, although every community stored these in their own armoury, to be removed only when needed.

In the meantime, monthly training days kept us all prepared and competent, just in case.

As a precaution, I always carried my personal weapons when travelling across country to the base. Robberies occasionally happened on remote routes, but these were becoming very rare, as anyone who committed such acts found themselves vigorously pursued by groups of well-trained, heavily armed and angry volunteer community members.

"Is Daisy excited about coming along with you?" Allan asked.

"Yes, of course she is. Although I think she's more excited about seeing that young lad who visited last year. I don't know how they managed it, but he's accompanying the South Wales council member to the base."

I gave him a severe look.

"If I didn't know any better I'd suspect that some unauthorised radio use has been allowed. But as that's your department, I can't possibly imagine that you'd let that happen. After all, a good friend wouldn't let my precious daughter go behind my back and make all these arrangements, would he?"

He winked. "No way I'd allow that, my friend. But to be fair, sometimes it's seemed as if forces that were beyond my control have been causing me to leave the radio room unattended. I'm not blaming your wife or my wife, but I think we may have been duped! Sorry."

I sighed. "Oh well, I can always fall back on the traditional 'scare the hell out your daughter's boyfriend' routine. It's so much easier now we have guns."

I half laughed, not even sure myself if I was serious or not. "I know I can trust you and Harry to look after things in my absence."

I looked up at the sound of laughter. Harry, and Kim, who was also pregnant again, had joined Stanley's group of friends.

As I looked at them, I couldn't help thinking now that some of us were getting older, that the group I was looking at included the most likely candidates to be taking over the country's leadership in the coming years. I looked round at the groups of people gathering around the large fire, and saw the faces of some of the original inhabitants of the community we had created, all those years ago.

Pete: the backbone of the community, despite his advancing years. He was still working alongside Michelle day after day, producing the lists and rotas that kept everyone working collectively and efficiently.

Mary: who still ran the community's school.

Jerry and Fiona: without my chance meeting with him in a cash and carry warehouse at the very beginning, I doubt if we would have survived six months. They still worked as doctor and dentist for our community and those around us.

Much of Jerry's time these days was spent treating injuries resulting from the manual labour that took up most of our days. The study he had begun at the start, to see if the change of diet and improved fitness regime we had been forced to follow as a result of our new circumstances would improve general health, had proved conclusively that it did.

The stores of regular antibiotics and traditional drugs had long ago run out, so he now spent the rest of his time consulting with Chris Garland, and studying the natural remedies that were available in the surrounding area. Combining this research with his knowledge of modern medicine, he had been very successful in coming up with remedies and concoctions to keep us healthy.

Other people milled around the fire. I spotted Chris Garland with his partner and a young family of his own.

All my friends were there, but they had become much more than friends; they were my extended family.

"Come on Allan, let's go and dance with our wives. We've got a lot to celebrate."

The Present Day

I snapped myself out of my daydream.

It had all seemed so real.

I sat and thought about my vision of the future for a while.

A warm glow spread though me. I knew that whatever happened, it was going to be all right. We were all going to prosper, grow and thrive from now on.

The worst of it was over. We'd survived attacks, famine, disease and much more.

We'd grown from a few neighbours and friends into a strong, secure community, more than capable of feeding and protecting itself. We had reached out to help others and been instrumental in getting the country back on its feet.

I thought about the part I had played in all this.

I thought about my frantic preparations before the event: amassing supplies, weapons and knowledge to help my family survive.

Then realising that there was strength in numbers, and deciding to help my immediate friends and neighbours.

Those few decisions in the early days had led all the way to a wedding attended by members of the royal family and the prime minister, and presided over by the Queen.

You couldn't make it up!

I had asked myself a question at the very start of this story.

"Am I a Prepper?"

You know what? I think I probably am.

Not from the Author

Dear Reader

I do hope you enjoy reading this book, but I feel I should warn you that, unlike my series UK DARK, which contains few profanities and limited descriptive violence, this book is different.

For the sake of realism there are frequent uses of the "F word" and the violence and gore is obviously more graphic. If this upsets you, then I am sorry, but in my defence, I think you would be hard pressed to find anyone under imminent threat of being eaten by a zombie who wouldn't swear profusely!

Thank you for your understanding.

ZOMBIE CASTLE:
ZC1

Chapter one

Wolfe medical research laboratory
Birmingham, England

"It works, it bloody works! Yes! We've done it!" Professor Andy Lawrence shouted, his eyes fixed on the screen in front of him.

He was Chief Scientist at Wolfe Medical, a small, privately funded research laboratory where the past eight years had been spent striving to develop a genetically modified "virus killer". Thousands of failed attempts had been made to develop a carefully altered rhinovirus (common cold virus) that would attach itself to a living virus in a cell and turn it into a harmless replica of itself. This process would continue until all virus cells were destroyed.

It would then lie dormant in the body until another strain of the rhinovirus was detected, when it would spring into action, modifying itself to match the new variant and starting all over again.

On the screen, small spiky blobs could be seen meeting and linking with other spiky blobs and then moving off to begin the process again.

"This," said Andy, "is the twentieth different serotype this beauty has attacked and rendered harmless."

His "second in command", Professor Ian Devey, sat beside him and stared at the screen, lost for words. More staff gathered round as word spread quickly around the laboratory.

This was the Holy Grail of viral research, Nobel Prize winning medicine, and they were all part of it. Careers had been made by moments like this. Once the silent wonder of what they were witnessing had passed, and realisation of their achievement had sunk in, the celebrations began.

The serious lab technicians and research assistants abandoned their usual reserve and began to cheer and clap. Shouting to make himself heard over the noise, Ian shook Andy's hand, "You must tell Mr Wolfe, he needs to know about this."

Andy shook his head, "I can't yet, Ian. I need to run more tests. Come on man, you know good research can't be rushed. I'll tell him as soon as we're sure it really works. We both know what he's like. He only wants positive results, not maybes. Another couple of months or so and then we'll tell him."

Disappointed, Ian nodded, "Of course, let's not get his hopes up. Shall we call it a day? It's two o'clock on a Friday afternoon. We won't get this lot back to work, so let's all finish early and I'll buy the first round in the pub."

"If you promise to buy the second one as well, I'll get this place cleared in ten minutes," Andy replied grinning.

Later on in the pub, Rose, one of the research assistants, typed a short message into her mobile phone, pressed send and put the phone back into her pocket. No one took any notice. Why would they? Texting was such a normal everyday activity.

Looking back, it was this moment that began the process by which human beings would cease to be the dominant species on the planet, and would become the hunted.

Printed in Great Britain
by Amazon